The Hunt

Alexa Filler

Copyright © 2024 by Alexa Filler

All rights reserved.

No portion of this book may be reproduced in any form without written permission from the publisher or author, except as permitted by U.S. copyright law.

Contents

When the Cop meets the Foreigner

I t all happened pretty quickly. Lame, I know.

One day, I was living a completely normal life. I was your typical junior in high school, getting mainly C's and trying to come with new excuses to not run the mile in gym. And then that all changed when my dad announced that not only had he gotten a promotion at work, but he was getting transferred to Sapporo. I can tell you one thing, that's not in America...Japan.

I'm not going to lie, at first I was bummed. I still am, I didn't want to leave anything behind. I loved living in San Francisco where all my friends were and where they spoke friggin' English. I was going to miss the life that I had here. I didn't know how to say anything in Japanese except thank you, Mr. Roboto— and I'm willing to bet that won't blow over very well in Japan. Dad did tell me that there was an English-language school there, but that hardly calmed my nerves. Still, because I was only seventeen, I flew across the Pacific Ocean to go live in a different country where I would feel like a complete outsider.

My dad didn't give me any absolution to not go to Japan. He just said that we were going and that was final. I was mad, and furious even he didn't care about how I felt about moving to a different country. All he cared about was his business, my dad only gave me two days to pack my things and we were off. He had his plane tickets already in hand while we headed out the door towards the airport.

As we boarded our flight and sat in our seats my dad decided to give one of his so called pep talks.

"Look son, I know we haven't been pretty close since your mother died...."

No shit.

"But, you have to give this a shot. Maybe try to learn a new language, it'll look good on your college application."

I was screaming on the inside and he didn't care. He let out a deep breathe, as he laid something on my lap making me arch my brow at it.

"All about Japan? History, language, and culture?" I asked him with a raised brow as he shrugged his shoulders.

"You might need it, its your first time in Japan. And we'll be here for awhile... just a little while until we go back. Who knows you might like it here...maybe even make some interesting new friends." I rolled my eyes at that easy for him to say, he's been there longer than I have and he already spoke the language. I glanced at him from the corner of my eye and noticed that he was already wearing his business suit. That meant that he was going to take off for work the minute we get settled into our new house.

As the plane docked, my dad was already making his business calls in Japanese and I didn't understand a word he said. People were staring at us everywhere we went but my dad didn't seem to notice. He was too busy and we just got here...great. With one hand and his luggage in the other he waved at the taxi guy who was already waiting for us. He bowed to us, making me arch my brow at that. I was never bowed at back at home...that was interesting.

"Hello, welcome to Japan." He said to me, noticing that my dad was too busy with the phone. I nodded back at him.

"Thanks."

"Let me get those bags for you." He said as he grabbed our luggage and we went inside the car. The city was huge when we drove through it and there was so much traffic, people were everywhere I looked and I couldn't help but take some pictures with my camera of the tall buildings that passed us, eventually, we pulled up into a quiet neighborhood.

Our brand new house looked really modern and was much larger than some of the other homes in the city thanks to my dad's affluent position at work. I was the first to get out of the cab and take a look around, anxious to explore it. I took a room upstairs with a large window that allowed me to get a glimpse of city life whenever I wanted.

At first, I considered just shutting myself away in my bedroom so that I wouldn't have to experience culture shock. However, I realized that maybe my dad was right, this would be a great opportunity to learn new things and experience a totally brand new way of life. And worse case scenario: if I didn't like living in Japan, then I just move back to the States after I graduate high school. As preparation for my new home, I 'd forced myself to watch some Japanese tutorial videos on YouTube, but I hardly considered myself fluent or even skilled in conversational Japanese. But what better way to learn than to immerse myself in the culture?

That was why I decided to venture out of our house the second day I was in Japan. My dad had already gone off work, so he wouldn't care if I left or not. I'd already adjusted to the massive time difference thanks to that trick of taking sleeping pills once the sun goes down. Meanwhile, my parents were struggling to get out of bed after the massive move and after feeling like it was the middle of the night during the day. Therefore, I went to walk around Sapporo by myself.

Downtown was just like any picture of the Japanese cities that I'd seen in magazines. There were sprawling skyscrapers built close together with large, neon signs displaying words in Katakana that I had no clue what they were saying. Since it was winter, there was a thick sheet of blackened snow along the road and sidewalk, and I kept my arms securely wrapped around myself in a feeble attempt to stay warm. I took in all the sights, smells, sounds. It was amazing, almost on par with living back in San Francisco.

My stomach began to grumble and I foolishly looked around for a McDonald's or something familiar that I could eat. Sure I like sushi, but I really desired something warm in the cold weather. I glanced around for a picture of food or something but frowned when I realized that a majority of the signs and posters were in Katakana, preventing me from understanding just what was going on. Dammit! The sidewalk was full of people, but all of them seemed to be on a mission, speeding past me at a quick pace before I could ask someone for directions to a fast food place or somewhere I could get a coffee something to help my stomach and warm me up.

The bitter air numbed my face and I frantically hurried up along the icy path. Pretty soon, all of the streets and buildings began to look the same. The winding sidewalks seemed to blend in with one another and it didn't take a genius to tell that I was completely lost.

"Oh crap," I muttered to myself, yanking my phone out of my pocket to dial my dad. However, because I was totally lazy, I hadn't gotten a Japanese SimCard yet, so my phone had a "No Service" signal flashing on the screen. Oh shit... this was bad. I was lost in Hokkaido's largest city without knowing the language and without anything in my stomach. Of course, this would happen to me. I was never known for my good luck.

I let out a sigh but I continued on my way, trying to retrace my steps, but it felt so futile trying to find my way home. All of the street maps were in Katakana, preventing me from even memorizing the names. I tried to remember certain symbols, figuring that one locked like half of a smiley face and another like window... but then what order were they in? Dammit! I was so utterly and completely lost.

I tried to look around for someone who could help me. "Ex-excuse me?" I asked one business-looking man.

But he kept on his way, not even giving me a second glance.

Okay...

I tried a couple more people, only to have then ignore me or not understand what I was saying. Alright, so maybe YouTube wasn't the way to try to learn the language. Still, my resolve to eat something or to get home only strengthened and I continued on my way through Downtown.

After a couple more minutes of freezing my ass off, I saw a police car that was pulled over to the side of the road. Perhaps the police could help me out with directions, or at least give me a ride home. Nervously, mainly because I didn't want the cop to think that I was bothering him, I shuffled my way towards the cruiser. Right in front of it was a policeman who was writing out a ticket for a sports car whose meter had expired.

The officer was crazy tall, towering over me. And he must've worked out a lot because his muscles strained against his tight blue uniform. On his right pec flashed a silver badge that gleamed in the cold sunlight. He wore a stern expression on his face as he scribbled whatever on the ticket before placing it on the windshield of the car. Then he turned around and spotted my awkward self standing a couple of feet away, twirling my fingers in front of me as I struggled to remember how to ask for help in Japanese. Man, if I could go back in time, I would've taken Japanese classes back in the States instead of Spanish.

The officer turned to face me, cocking his eyebrow at me in confusion at first. However once our eyes locked, his features softened and his jaw dropped in shock for a brief second. He shook his head and cleared his throat. He started mumbling something in his language, his voice was deep and authoritative. Manly and full of dominance.

I arched my brow and tried snapping myself out of my daze as I could feel myself blush at my ignorance of the language here. "I'm sorry, I do not understand Japanese," I said speaking slowly, using one of the few phrases that I'd memorized. "Do you speak English?" I asked him hesitantly.

The officer's dark eyes lit up as they ran up and down my shivering body while a small smirk formed on his lips and he gave a curt nod. "Yes, I speak English," he answered, an accent barely audible. Maybe he spent some time in America? "Was there anything I can I help you with?"

I barely contained my excitement at having found someone who I could understand. "Oh thank God!" I cheered, unconsciously closing the space between us, which only seemed to highlight the height difference between us. The cop had a good foot on me. But maybe I could finally make one friend here in Japan. "I just moved here and I got completely lost. I was wondering if you could give me directions to the neighborhood in block Thirty-Two? If it's not too much of a hassle, please."

"I know where that is," the officer grinned, sending a shiver down my spine. He was so handsome, and I was also a sucker for a man in uniform. What? I couldn't help it... "If you would like, I could give you a ride to where you need to be." He gestured at the cruiser with his gloved hand. Wow, a man in uniform who spoke English and now a break from the harsh winter weather? Things were finally starting to look up for me. Maybe life in a foreign country wouldn't be so bad after all. "Thank you!" I gushed, scurrying over to the passenger side of the police car.

The officer chuckled. "I think that's the first time I've seen anyone eager to get into my car," he laughed as he unlocked the car, settling in behind the wheel.

I hopped inside and did my seatbelt. I hardly ever wore one, but I figured that I should when in the company of the law. "Thank you again for your help," I said as he pulled away from the curb and sped down the road. "I haven't quite gotten the hang of Japanese yet."

The officer nodded. "It's no problem," he said, flashing me a grin, making me blush. "Besides, it's my job to protect the citizens of Sapporo. And that includes you, too." He said with a smirk.

Trying to warm myself up, I put my hands close to the heater, feeling my fingers gradually thaw out in the wonderful warm air. "If you don't mind me asking," I was really prying by now, "how did you learn English? You speak it very good."

"I speak it very well," the cop corrected, wagging his finger at me in a condescending motion. Making me once again blush furiously. "I worked at Misawa Air Base with some of the Americans when I was in the Self-Defense Forces. I picked up a majority of them and the rest I learned when I was in school."

"Well, hopefully, I can pick up on Japanese really quickly," I said. "That way, I won't have to distract you from your work anymore." I gave a light-hearted chuckle at the end of my corny statement.

The officer gave his own throaty chuckle. "It's no bother, really," he reassured me, reaching over and running a warm hand over my cheek...woah... what? I quickly moved out of his way because it just made me feel awkward. The handsome officer frowned at that and closed his hand in the air but he somehow dismissed my movement. "And as for the language barrier, I can easily act as your translator. Its no trouble really just doing my duty as an officer. Helping out their citizens in a time of need." He flashed me a smile.

I'd rather learn than just have to go through someone twenty-four/seven. Plus, it'd be a total invasion of my privacy, having the officer literally know everything that's going on in my life because I'd have to have him around all the time in order to communicate with others. I also couldn't help but find it a little weird how this officer was suddenly so interested in me. Instead of voicing my opinion to the nice stranger, I just nodded. After all, I didn't want to seem rude to neglect his offer.

"Yeah," I muttered, having nothing else really to say on the matter. A part of me was still pretty shocked at how he'd stroked my cheek all nonchalantly. That wasn't a custom here, right?

"And, forgive me if I'm prying," the officer said, believe me I did that already…"but what were you doing out on the streets of Sapporo all by yourself?"

"I thought that I'd tried to explore some of the city," I answered, looking out the window as he drove, trying to memorize the path he was taking. "But then I got hungry and couldn't find a café anywhere. And that's when I got lost."

"Mm-hmm," the officer hummed before taking a sharp u-turn, making me flail against my door.

"Wha—?"

"There's a café down the street this way," he said, knowing that I was confused by his actions. "I can take you there, and then I'll drive you home afterwards. Sound good?"

It honestly sounded like a fantastic idea! I was so cold that a hot chocolate or a hot cup of coffee sounded like Heaven. "Yeah," I agreed. "Thanks for showing me around, by the way."

"Anytime."

When we arrived, the café was a Western-style coffee shop that had small round tables with actual chairs, not one of those kneeling tables and matts that I've seen on anime. Huh, so apparently watching a crap ton of anime was also not the best way to prepare for my move to Japan. Utilizing the hot policeman's translating, I ordered a hot chocolate from the barista and when I pulled some yen out of my wallet, the officer put his hand up to me.

"I got it," he smiled, paying for both of our drinks.

"Oh, you didn't have to do that," I muttered, feeling a little guilty for using him for a ride and now a hot beverage. Wow, the police here really do take care of the citizens. Were all of the officers in Japan this civil?

He didn't say anything, and instead took both of our mugs over to a far table that was next to the window. I took at seat that had me facing the wall, while he took the one that allowed him to overlook the rest of the restaurant so that there was no one behind him. Once he placed my mug in front of me, I was surprised to see that he must've ordered me a children's drink because there was a cat-shaped marshmallow floating in it. I was seventeen, not five.

"Thank you," I said, trying to be polite. It was free after all.

"Don't mention it," he grinned, taking a sip of his adult looking coffee with no cartoonish candies in it.

Biting down my disappointment at coming off as a child, I took a small sip of the hot drink, marveling at its sweet deliciousness. It was so good!

Okay, so maybe I would have to order the cat drink next time I come here. Secretly, of course.

"So you must be attending the International High School, am I correct?" the officer asked.

I nodded after taking a loud gulp of my drink, the cat now a melted glob of white stickiness that I could feel on my upper lip. "Yeah," I answered, wiping my mouth with a napkin real quick, "my dad said that they teach exclusively in English there. And they offer beginner courses on Japanese, so I can learn how to get around town better."

He frowned, furrowing his brow. "Don't worry about the language," he urged, his voice a little rougher than usual. "The police are all supposed to be fluent in English, so whenever you need help, you just give me a call."

Weird... "Um, well I never transferred my phone," I said meekly. "So that won't really work. I need to go to the store to get a Japanese SimCard, but I need one of my dad's phones because it's under his name." Speaking of which, I really needed to get that done sooner rather than later so that I could watch some videos using my data while in math class.

The police officer nodded again, silently thinking to himself for a moment. He seemed to be really intense, his light colored eyes staying glued to my body the whole time he considered whatever he was thinking about. Truth be told, it was kind of uncomfortable to be under the watchful and scrutinizing gaze of the older, more powerful man. I squirmed in my seat and quickly downed my drink, hoping to come up with an excuse to go home. Sure, the cop was nice to look at, but there was this voice in my back of my skull that told me to keep my guard up. I'm not exactly sure why; however, my mom raised me with the belief to always trust my gut. And right now, my gut was telling me to go home.

"Well, that was really good," I said, setting my empty mug down on the table. "But I really must get going."

The officer snapped out of whatever trance he was in, shaking his head a little bit. "Oh, y-yeah, I'll drive you to your house," he said.

"That won't be necessary...I can really just take the bus." The officer shook his head. "No, no allow me please. I insist."

I still couldn't brush off he feeling about being a little creeped out by his eager to help me out. But I ignored it, I didn't want to over think this too much. After all he was just an officer helping out a civilian. Even if he was being overly friendly about it.

We exited the café and got back into his cramped police cruiser. After telling him my address, he quickly found my new house, pulling up into the driveway next to Dad's car.

"Thank you very much for the ride, and the snack," I said, unbuckling my seatbelt. I felt bad that I didn't do anything for him in return. He's been nothing but kind to me, and I didn't want him to think that I was being an ignorant American. "Um, I can give you some gas money?" I told him automatically reaching for my pocket.

He scoffed and waved his large at me again, stopping me from making any further movement. "There's no need," he smiled, his pearly whites huge and predatory like. "Just glad I could help. And by the way, I'm Tanaka Raizo." He pointed at the name tag on his beefy chest, but because it was in Katakana, I just took his word for it.

"I'm Lark, like the songbird," I said, blushing a little bit at the name that my nature-loving mom cursed me with. Why couldn't she had given me a badass name, like Max Powers or Rad-Blaster?

Raizo's smile grew even large now, his wide eyes glimmering in the sunlight. "Nice to meet you, Lark," he grinned.

I wasn't too familiar with Japanese honorifics, but I knew that "-san" was a pretty common way of showing respect. "Nice to meet you too, Tanaka-san," I said, hoping that I'd gotten it right by attaching the suffix to his surname. Man, I really needed to sign up for that Japanese course at school, no matter what Raizo thought. Speaking of which, it was rather odd that he didn't seem too keen on me learning the language of his country that I was currently living in. I couldn't shake the feeling that that was some kind of ploy or prank, or something.

He opened his mouth to say something, but then closed it, an almost evil-looking grin forming. "Actually," he smirked, his deep voice giddy and eager, "there's a special term utilized for police officers. It's just a respect-thing, so use it to blend into society and address me as such in public."

"Oh, okay," I said, feeling a little bit like I was being chided. "What is it?" I really did want to know so that I didn't come off looking like an even bigger ignorant American than I already was. He said the word slowly, as if speaking to a child.

"Otousan?" I repeated slowly letting the word wrap around my tounge, wondering why it sounded a lot like something I'd heard on a non-dubbed anime that didn't have a police character in it. But I guess there's only so many syllabic sounds mankind can come up with, so some words were bound to be alike.

"That's right," he smirked, puffing out his chest with pride, looking just proud of himself. His eyes gleamed with pride when he looked at me.

"Oh, um, okay," I muttered. "Thanks for the lesson, otousan." I have to be honest: it sounded awkward rolling off my tongue and made me feel like even more a child around the older man as I struggled. But still if it was what the police officer was instructing me to call him, I suppose it was correct. Why would an officer of the law lie to me? I pulled open the door and began to get out of the car. "Thanks again for the ride."

Raizo continued to grin my way, giving me a little wave. "See you around, Lark!" he called.

I nodded. "Bye, otousan!" I skipped up the steps to the front door of my house, slamming the door shut behind me once I was inside. I heard the police cruiser speed off down the street, and I went about the rest of the day inside the safety of my walls, trying to get over the nice/weird feelings that I'd gotten from Raizo, or otousan. Afterall, i'm not gay. Just because I admit that he is a little goodlooking didn't mean anything. Whatever the heck that meant... I don't know why, but I was a little on edge when around him, almost as if there was something that I needed to be on the lookout for.

A/N: I'm trying something new, and yes another werewolf story sue me. Let me know what you guys think! Also, I will be re-publishing my accidentally deleted book "Kiss of Death" soon. So stay tuned. :)

First times the charm

Tanaka Raizo:

Do I believe in love at first sight? Yes. And on top of that, I definitely know that Lark and I share a bond that goes beneath the surface of other relationships. Intuitively, I could sense our connection that was stronger than steel— unbreakable and uncontrollable. Plus, we have the best dynamic: Lark-kun needs me in order to survive in Sapporo.

The very moment that I laid my eyes on him, I knew that he was mine.

I'd been busy writing a parking ticket when I glanced up and looked into the eyes of an angel, all shy and innocent. Just the way he appeared so lost and afraid of the large city made me feel this indescribable urge to protect him and shield him away from the rest of the world. And when I began to speak to Lark-kun, I was amazed by his eagerness to learn about and explore his new home. And his voice was soft and gentle, like a wind chime that eased my soul and seemed to make all the worries of the day evaporate into nothingness. His Japanese was terrible, but that only sparked something inside of me, my brain formulating some ideas that could work in my favor.

I gave Lark-kun a ride to a café, buying him a cute drink that made me think of him because they were both adorable. Afterwards, I drove him home, memorizing the exact location just in case I had to come back real soon. The best part of all was that I even convinced him to refer to me as "Otousan", my insides doing flips as soon as the name left his smooth lips. Thanks to his lack of knowledge regarding the Japanese language, he had no clue that I'd tricked him into calling me Daddy; and he didn't need to know until I made my move. All I had to do was make sure that no one else moved in on my territory so that I can properly court him. Then he'll agree to be all mine forever.

I watched as Lark-kun skipped inside his house, waiting until I saw him close the front door. Call it my protective instincts that arise due to my job as a police officer, but I just wanted to make sure that he was inside his new house, safe and sound.

And now it was time to put my plan into action.

I sped down the street, weaving among the numerous buildings and blocks until I reached the koban that I was assigned to. It was only a five minute drive from Lark-kun's house, so that meant that I wouldn't have to drive far in order to see him, which brought a large smile to my face. Once I pulled up in front of the koban, I jumped out and hurried inside, eager to enact Phase One of my plan to win over my boy.

"Hey, Tanaka-san!" my colleague, Satō Koichi, called as soon as I walked in. He smiled and gave me a small wave. He'd just been transferred to Sapporo from Mikasa, which was significantly smaller. Therefore, he still had that small-town charm about him: very helpful and not asking too many questions whenever I gave him directions.

I started to head towards the back door where we kept all of our supplies. "Satō-san, I have to go have a talk with Fujioka," I said. "Do you think you still have a hold over things here?"

"Fujioka?" Satō-san asked, cocking his eyebrow at me. "Why do you need to speak to him?"

"I, um, got a complaint that he was hassling some shopkeeper earlier today," I lied. "So I figured I'd give him a stern talking-to before anything escalates."

"Would you like some backup?" He mused.

"No, thank you!" I called, entering the storage room in the back, shuffling through the multitudes of supplies that were at my disposal. Now sure, someone who might have been observing me would claim that I was nuts to be pining over some high schooler who I just met, but they didn't understand the extent to which my desire lies. Also, Lark was new in Japan, and as an officer, it was my duty to protect the citizens of Sapporo. Hence, it was my responsibility to keep an eye on him— therefore, I was just going above and beyond in my job performance. That's how I rationalized it as I grabbed the cardboard box that had the surveillance cameras and bugging devices.

I had to make sure to hurry that way I could get to Fujioka before he left to go do something stupid... again. Fujioka was the son of the one of the higher ups in the local yakuza clans in Sapporo. He could usually be found at one of the bars that he owned in the Susukino district, and thanks to my turning a blind eye to some of his activities, he knew that he owed me a favor. And it was time to collect.

Once again, Satō-san looked confused when he saw me exit the back room with the large cardboard box in my hands. He opened his mouth to ask a question, but I beat him to it before he could utter a syllable.

"The koban in the next neighborhood requested some other supplies," I called over my shoulder as I left the building. I shoved the box into my trunk and hightailed it over to Susukino, making it rather quickly thanks to the grid-like way that Sapporo was designed. When compared to other cities in Japan, it was fairly easy for foreigners to navigate. So the fact that my poor Lark-kun got lost in it only highlights how much he needs me.

The very second my cruiser was parked in front of the bar that Fujioka owned, a couple of his cronies, clad in their usual business suits, came outside. Their eyes were glued on me as I exited my car, their postures stiff and alert as if I posed some kind of threat to their boss. I fought my scowl that wanted to take over my face.

"I'm here to see Fujioka-san," I sneered at them, straightening my own posture and flashing my badge at them. "Is he available?"

The largest of the group took a small step forward, cracking his knuckles in front of him. "Do you have an appointment?" he asked in a rough-sounding voice. They were trying to intimidate me, but it wouldn't work. I was a decorated police officer, notorious for never backing down. They knew that I'd arrested several of their own members over the years, so that was probably the only reason as to why they didn't outright jump me right now.

"I don't need an appointment," I said, crossing my arms in front of myself, making sure to flex my large biceps as I did so. "Now, are you going to take me to him, or do I need to bring some guys down here to make sure all of your licensing is up to code?"

The goon's face turned red and his vein throbbed out on his forehead as he clenched his jaw. "Right this way," he growled through clenched teeth.

I followed behind him into the dimly-lit bar, chuckling at the way some of the patrons tried their best to not make eye-contact with me. I was led into the back room where Fujioka sat at a desk, his feet perched up high on the furniture as he looked over some papers, looking bored to death. When he noticed me enter his office, he didn't even flinch of make a face.

"You wanna know something?" he droned, his voice slow and painfully monotone. "I really miss the days when I would get to beat the shit outta some fool who didn't pay for his protection. But now, all 'cause of the upstanding police presence we have in Sapporo, I'm limited to doing business behind a desk." He narrowed his eyes at me and then returned to stare blankly at the papers in front of him.

"Well then I guess you'll enjoy what I'm about to tell you," I said, smirking as soon as I saw his lip twitch in interest.

"I'm listening," he said, tossing the papers to the side where the rustled to the hardwood floor.

I took a step forward, slowly approaching his desk. "There's this new family that moved into the Thirty- Block," I told him, placing both of my hands firmly on the wooden desk. "An American family with a son. I want you to gather some information for me."

He rolled his eyes. "That's it?" he scoffed, leaning back in his chair. "Really? That's the favor you're gonna' cash in?" He ran a thick hand through his messy hair.

Ignoring him for the moment, I continued on. "You're going to tell me where the boy's parents work, how long they're there, and how long the boy is left unattended. And then, you're going to get the boy's school schedule and find out exactly where he sits in every class."

A faint glimmer sparkled in Fujioka's eye. "Oh," he mused, tapping his mouth a little bit. "So, Sapporo's rough-n-tough cop has a crush on a little gaijin? How sweet." He droned, with a click of his tongue.

"Have you told him that yet though?" He teased.

I clenched my jaw and slammed my heavy hands back down on the desk, making his goon behind me take a loud step forward. "I'm serious, Fujioka," I sneered. "You need to tell me everywhere my boy goes, who he's hanging out with, and what his interests are. And most importantly, you need to make sure he never goes out with another guy, or girl and if he does, I need you to report it to me immediately. Understand?"

"Yeah, yeah," he chuckled, stretching his hands behind his head. "So tell me, what makes this... American so special?" He took a pause until his eyes sparkled in recognition.

"Unless he's...."

"He's mine," I simply stated. "And I need to do everything in my power to keep him."

Lark :

My alarm went off so early that it should've been illegal. Groaning, I slammed the machine quiet and crawled out of bed, grimacing that the sun was barely rising. Why did school have to start so early here? As if moving wasn't bad enough, but I had to go to a completely new school that would be filled with new faces. I consider myself a little shy at first and I really needed to make some friends if I wanted to survive in Japan. I couldn't just hang out with my parents or a policeman for the entirety of my teen years.

Speaking of which, I had trouble getting Raizo out of my head. Thoughts of the helpful and sexy cop filtered into my brain every few seconds. Despite being a genuinely nice man, he gave me some creeper vibes that told me to stay on my toes when around him. But I'm sure that it was just my overactive imagination and nothing to worry too much about, right?

I showered and got dressed in my uniform which consisted of a white button-down shirt and black slacks, making me look like a complete nerd. I grimaced as I stared at myself in the mirror, wishing that I could just wear a hoodie and some jeans, but whatever. I yanked on a school-approved jacket that was gray and had no logos on it. Zipping it up all the way to my neck, I swung my backpack over my shoulder and slumped down the stairs where I saw my dad in the kitchen, sipping some coffee.

"Hey, Lark!" he smiled at me, sounding way too chipper for this time of day. "Ready for your first day at a brand-new school?"

"Oh yeah," I muttered. "I can't wait." The thought of having to go to an entirely new school in the middle of the school year made me want to throw up. Plus, I'd heard the stories about how rigorous and dedicated the students are in Japan. I'm not saying I'm a slacker, but...yeah, I'm a slacker. So I'll be at the bottom of my class!

My dad shook his head, rubbing his temples. "Just try to give it a chance," he groaned. "Who knows, there may be something here in Japan that will just take hold of you. And then you'll never leave."

Yeah, maybe. "I guess you're right," I mumbled, grabbing an orange off the counter. "Can you drive me today? I got so lost yesterday and I don't want to be late for my first day." Memories of wandering the large city all confused and alone made me feel nauseas; plus, Raizo had warned me that the transit system here was a nightmare. So I figured that my dad driving me would be the best option.

He nodded and grabbed for his keys. "Sure, I can give you a lift today," he agreed. "But we have to leave now if I'm going to make it work on time."

I happily followed my dad outside of the house, eagerly jumping into his car. Of course I wasn't excited to have to be going to school, I was relieved to not have to take the bus or get another awkward ride from a police officer. I tried to memorize the path that my dad drove, taking in which building was where and which corner to turn down. As we were going, I noticed that there was a black car with tinted windows following behind us, taking every turn that we were. Maybe it was one of my new classmates?

"So, you're going to have to take the bus home or walk," my dad said. "Your mother has to work late and I get off after your school lets out."

I nodded. "Okay," I said, already feeling a little apprehensive about having to navigate the large city on my own again. When I'd gotten home yesterday, I'd asked my parents to get me a Japanese SimCard so that I could use my phone again, and they said that they'd have to do it later— later meaning today after work. So at least I'd have my phone tomorrow to call people in case of an emergency, but that didn't help me out today.

Sighing, I guessed that if things came down to worst, then I could just keep an eye out for Raizo to give me a ride home again. I just hoped that he wouldn't think of me as needy and get fed up. But there was something in the back of my skull that told me that I could count on him.

Otousan seemed like an okay guy; creepy, but okay.

"Dad?" I asked him... making him hum under his breath.

"Can I ask you something?"

"Aren't you already?"

I scoffed at that.

"What does otousan mean in Japanese?" I asked him hesitantly making him arch a brow as he glanced at me at the corner of his eye as he tried to keep his eyes on the road.

"Already trying to impress me with your language skills? It means father ...or daddy." Daddy? A furious blush tickled at the base of my neck, why would that officer want me to call him...daddy!? Is he a part of a cult?

I swallowed that thought down as I tried not to think too hard about it. He can't be...maybe its just a term of endearment or a part of the culture.

The International High School was a bit of a drive away from the house, so it would be smarter to take a bus home afterwards. Dad dropped me off in front and I stared up at the large, intimidation building that was two story and looked more like a university than a high school. Taking a deep breath to calm my timid nerves, I walked inside and was grateful to see a majority of the signs in English. My dad had told me that this high school taught exclusively in English because a lot of the local students wanted to learn so that they could study and travel abroad. Wow, talk about dedication to education.

After picking up my schedule in the office, and doing under cartwheels of joy that the staff spoke to me in English that was more proper than mine, I went to my first class. I was a little happy that I was enrolled in the Japanese-language class where I'd be able to learn the language. That way, I wouldn't be so lost and dependent on the kindness of strangers. I wasn't a child anymore, so I needed to learn how to fend for myself. I liked to feel independent. And a course that taught me the land's language would help me to assert that.

Because I'm shy and I also don't want it to be too obvious that I don't pay a lot of attention to lessons, I took a seat near the back of the classroom. And speaking of the classroom, it was awfully plain and just had several rows of wooden desks lined up in front of a larger desk that had a green chalkboard behind it. I could feel my heart dropping as I realized that this school was going to be much more serious about lectures and actual learning than my last one, where I had a study hall period in which my friends and I would just go to McDonald's.

Once I was in my seat in the back, I tore my notebook out of my backpack to try to look like I was going to be a willing participant to school. I flipped sit open and began to copy whatever was written on the board: some left-over scribblings from yesterday about osmosis, the date, and a couple of Katakana characters that I totally butchered as I tried to rewrite them.

When class began, I was painfully aware that all of my assumptions were correct. The curriculum was extremely fast-paced when compared to my school back home in the States. I felt so lost and when the teacher called on me to answer a question, I'd always feel my face burn scarlet red as I'd simply answer: "I dunno'." It was rapidly becoming my catchphrase.

And damn, I thought that I'd excel in English class because it's my native language and all that. However, apparently my grammar ain't all fancy and shit, so I looked like an idiot when I was unable to determine whether the usage of "lie" or "lay" was appropriate in an example. Maybe I should just drop out and become a porn star...with a way below average body. Dammit! At least my instructors taught in English though otherwise I'd be a goner.

Luckily, lunchtime was after English, so that's give my poor brain a break from realizing that it was totally impaired (and that's putting it lightly). I'd packed my lunch at home, so I took a seat at one of the tables that was closest to a window. As I pulled apart my crummy sandwich, I stared outside at the snow that was falling, desperately wishing that I was back in California where I didn't eat alone and didn't feel so behind the curve. That's not to say there's no smart people in the States, but at least I wasn't considered super slow...just regular slow.

I sat alone at a table with my head in my hands, I was already a loner on the first day...great. I heard someone trying to talk to me in Japanese making my head slowly rise to look at him.

He walked up to my sad solo-table, holding a tray in his hands. I'd already had my first lesson in my Japanese class, but all I retained was that konnichiwa meant hello, and niji meant rainbow. So yeah, useful stuff. So given my utter lack of Japanese, I just stared blankly up at the guy at the table, feeling so incredibly stupid and pathetic.

The guy mumbled something again, his voice going slow as if he were speaking to a child.

Dammit... "I'm sorry, I do not speak Japanese," I said, using the most useful phrase in Japanese that I knew.

"Oh!" the guy exclaimed, setting his tray down at the table. "My bad. I should've guessed by the clueless look on your face."

Ouch, there goes my self-esteem. "Yeah, I just moved here," I said, nervously ripping the crust from my bread. "I still haven't mastered the language yet."

The boy nodded. "Don't worry about it," he assured me, digging into his own lunch. "They say that the best way to learn a new language is to immerse yourself into the culture."

Shoot, I really hope that's right, because there's no way I can spend a year and a half here walking around clueless until I graduated and got to move back to the States. That would be terrible.

"I'm Hajime by the way," the guy said, eagerly chewing on his food. He must've been really hungry.

"Lark," I grinned, happy that it looked like I was making a friend on my first day at school. Given my shy and quiet demeanor, I was willing to bet that it'd take me at least a week to get up the nerve to talk to someone. Luckily though, there were always some extroverts out there would initiate conversation; that was honestly how I made most of my friends.

"So how are you liking Japan?" Hajime asked, trying to make small talk.

"It's... different," I admitted. "I haven't quite gotten the hang of stuff yet. Like yesterday, I got so lost downtown and a policeman had to give me a lift home." I began to laugh at the end of my recount of meeting Raizo because once I allowed my nerves to calm down, it was a funny story to tell people.

Hajime must've thought it was funny too because he began to chuckle a little bit awkwardly along with me.

"Did you say...Raizo?"

"As in Tanaka Raizo?" He asked with an arched brow making me nod as I took a bite out of my sandwhich.

"Yeah! You know him?"

"I did...." He trailed off as if he didn't want to talk about him anymore which made me frown. How did he know Tanaka?

"Well, I'd be more than happy to show you around the city," he grinned, clearly trying to change the subject. "Unless you'd rather have the omawari-san help you out again."

"The what?" I wondered. What was an omawari-san? Judging by the honorific attached to the end, it was a person.

Hajime wrinkled his forehead at me. "A police officer," he said, sounding like it should've been obvious.

But that wasn't what Raizo told me to call him. He told me to call him something else...and as much as I was tempted to ask Hajime about it, I bit my tongue to swallow it down. "Um," I mused, "I thought it was...something else." I didn't want to say Otousan was wrong, because maybe there was more than one word for police officer in Japanese. Maybe the cop just liked going by different names. Perhaps Raizo let me in on a nickname that he had? Or maybe I had just misheard him, and he'd really said omawari-san? Regardless, I thought it best to just keep my mouth shut and enjoy the company of my new friend instead of looking like an even bigger dumbass.

After that school went on fairly...horrible for the rest of the day. My humiliation only continued to deepen as I had the notion that I was significantly behind the curve of other students here. My grades in America didn't help and everyone was already calling me the dumb white guy behind my back. Thanks to Hajime who kept me informed about it. Despite that, I tried to focus on the fact that I'd made a new friend in Hajime. He was a nice guy and liked to joke around a lot. And plus, he actually wanted to spend time with me, offering to even walk me home so that I wouldn't get lost. Even after I told him that it'd be easier to take the bus, he insisted on walking because I'd get to see more of Sapporo that way.

They did say, that when you made at least one friend on the first day of school you'd be okay for the rest of semester.

"So how are you liking life in Japan so far?" Hajime asked as they walked the busy streets of Japan back home.

"Its good I guess...better than I thought it would be. Honestly, I thought it was going to be worse but thanks to you its making it better." Hajime laughed at that.

"Yeah its no problem, listen I want to introduce you to some of my friends tomorrow who were so interested in meeting the new American at school. Everyone was talking about you before you came here." He said.

"Really? Wow, I'm honestly not that interesting to talk about." Hajime laughed.

"Maybe, to you... but when a new American shows up to school its always interesting for us no matter what. Be careful of who you make friends with though, most Japanese might just want to get to know you so that they can practice their English. Or take advantage of you."

He warned making me grimace.

"Thanks for the warning. I'll keep that in mind." As we stopped by the stoplight we noticed a cop coming toward us one that wasn't Raizo. It made me feel uneasy.

"Also, if you like I can teach you some Japanese with my friends sooner or later you'll pick it up the more exposed you are."

"That'll be great! Thanks Hajime."

"Sure...hey is it me or is that officer following us." Hajime said as he noticed who I was staring at.

The officer started shouting something at us and blew his whistle.

"Oh shit." Hajime cursed as the officer ran towards them.

"What is he saying!?" I asked nervously, we have to wait we can't outrun him. Hajime bit out as he held my arm in place.

The officer in front of us started yelling at Hajime while looking at me. What did he want?

Hajime yelled something back, and I couldn't help but feel nervous and stressed as people started staring at us curiously as they walked by. The officer suddenly slapped Hajime in the face making me gasp.

"Hey! What are you doing!?" I cried out to the officer who suddenly turned to me. "Papers!"

He said to me while holding his hand out to me.

"W-what papers? I-I don't understand."

Hajime held his face in his hand as he tried to explain to the officer. "I've been trying to tell him that you are still trying to get your legal papers registered in this country. In Japan you have to have them with you where you go. Even if you're just traveling, he's asking for any type of ID or passport. Its required for foreigners 24/7." He explained, "do you have yours on you?"

My hands started to get clammy as I dug my hand in my backpack but couldn't find them. Why didn't my dad tell me any of this before dropping me off to school!? I have my passport but its at home!

"I don't have them with me!" I cried out to him nervously, this couldn't be happening to me.

"Idiot American!" The officer cried as he went to strike me only for his hand to stop in mid-air making me flinch and close my eyes, bracing myself for the strike.

"Do not touch him! He's a visitor to Japan and doesn't know our customs!" A familiar deep voice growled out and made me slowly open my eyes as I saw Tanaka Raizo standing in front of me.

How?

Curiosity Killed the Cat

How was he just here? How is that possible?

One minute here I was, about to be arrested just for being a foreigner without papers. And the next, I was getting rescued by an oddly creepy cop who I think is stalking me.

Did he follow me? I instantly brushed that thought away. I didn't want to come to that conclusion it would only creep me out. I snapped myself out of my trance and looked at Raizo. For some reason, I got that weird sinking feeling that those two cops knew each other in the past, but not in a good way...I could tell that just by looking at them.

Raizo looked at the officer in front of him with a harsh glare on his face. And being the stupid kid I am...I stupidly opened my mouth like a gaping fish in shock at his sudden appearance. I was about to call him by his name when I remembered something he told me before.

Something he said that he wanted me specifically to call him by...and I knew that Hajime was going to laugh at me but it was the only thing I could think of to calm him down. So I did. I was probably going to hate myself for this, but it was the only way. "Otousan?" I said slowly, and very unsurely as I walked up to him and placed a hand on his arm. The cop in front of me visibly relaxed and puffed out his chest. Almost as if he looked unsually and deeply satisfied that I called him that in front of other people. By reflex, he smacked the other cops hand out of the way while stepping in front of me.

To my left, I heard Hajime choking back a laugh which made me frown. What was so funny? Did I say something wrong? Maybe I should have just called him by his first name. Isn't it a custom to call that the Japanese called their elders by otousan? Since he told me to call him that? Maybe not, maybe I shouldn't have said anything at all. Another blush tried come up my cheeks, but I fought it back down. I was turning into such a girl. The other cop barked out a laughter and said something in Japanese that sounded like it was meant to be offensive. Because he was looking at me and the other cop was making some kind of facial expression of disgust?

I instantly felt embarrassed as Hajime and the other cop laughed at me. As if sensing my embarrassment Raizo stood next to me with his arm touching mine. Somehow, him being that close made me feel not as embarrassed. And I didn't know why.

I cringed to myself. "So...tell me American how much money did you pay out to get in?" He spat. What did he mean?

Raizo let out a growl, and I literally

"That's enough leave him be Uchiha this is his first time here in Japan. Take it easy on him." Raizo said while puffing his chest out and standing in front of me. "I'll give him a warning and he'll be sure to have his passport on him next time." He said.

"No...unfortunately for you, i'm going to write him a warning." He said while taking out a notepad.

A warning!?

My dad is going to kill me.

"Uchiha... i'll give him the warning myself...your job here is done. Leave!" He said making Uchiha roll his eyes, he gave me one cold look before walking away. The crowd around us looked at us every now and then trying to figure out what was going on but they stopped and lost interest.

"You alright there Lark? You scared me for a second. Do I need to talk to your dad about not bringing the proper documentation around with you in Japan?" He asked while raising a brow at me, the way he talked to me though sounded like a father was accusing his child of doing something wrong. It made me feel like even more of a five-year-old when he talked to me like that, and i'd be lying if I said that it didn't annoy me.

"What's going to happen to you the next time I'm not there to save you?" He mused. Wait, did I hear that right?

"Come again? Next time? What makes you think that there's going to be a next time?" I challenged.

"Calm down, Lark he's just playing." Hajime said. I brushed him off, suddenly feeling embarrassed again.

"But to answer your question from before, I honestly didn't know about that, I have my passport and everything but I guess my dad forgot to remind me to bring that too..." I said awkwardly. He glanced at Hajime, as if he just noticed him for the first time and nodded to him in acknowledgment.

"Hajime... I see you're getting along with the new American." He said, making me blush while he never kept his gaze off of me. Again, creepy.

"Y-yeah sir, he just transferred to my academy lately."

"Good, would he be meeting the others?" Raizo asked him. Others? "I hope he'll be able to fit in with our culture and people."

"Don't worry, he would be and I plan on that, we haven't had the chance to introduce them to my friends," Hajime said shly. I don't know what is but a sudden string of silver hit my core at seeing them talk. It made me feel left out that these two somehow knew each other more than meets the eye.

"Well anyways, isn't it about time that you two went home? You both shouldn't be out here alone..."

"I was just planning on taking Lark home. Since his dad made him walk home, he doesn't know the way back." Hajime explained, all while trying to be a good civilian that he is.

"I see... you don't need to worry about that Hajime, I can take him from here." He answered, making my blood turn cold. Sure, at first when he tried helping me out I didn't mind it at all. In fact, I saw it as a good thing that he was going an extra mile on helping a foreigner. But now that he was turning up out of nowhere it was getting a bit too uncomfortable for me. Did he do this to all foreigners? Should I talk to my dad about this? Who am I kidding, my dad's so busy with work that he won't have time to even talk to me much less take a tour around Japan. We've never been close even when my mom used to be alive.

"Oh..okay sure then. You'll be much safer with a cop anyways. See you at school tomorrow Lark!" Hajime winked at me and did a quick bow to Raizo before taking off and passing through the thick crowd on the streets. Raizo flashed me a smile as I stood there awkwardly with my hands tucked safely into my pockets.

"So, did your dad give you a specific curfew?" He asked, making me scoff and roll my eyes.

"I'm not twelve." I mumbled, feeling slightly offended when he laughed.

"Oh, believe me I know that. I'm just surprised that he isn't very careful around you, you'll never know when someone might come along and snatch you up in Japan." He mentioned with an awkward laugh. Yeah, like you? I wanted to bite back but I kept my mouth shut. I didn't want to say or do anything stupid to provoke a cop like him. Who knows what he could do to me?

"You're right, it could be risky."

"I'm sure your dad wouldn't mind me showing you a tour around Japan? Why don't we walk around for a bit, and go sightseeing? Maybe even grab a bite to eat for dinner." I know he was just trying to be friendly but he was overdoing it to the point where red flags were going up. I gulped at his question, trying to dig my brain around for an excuse. I looked up and realized that that was a mistake, he was looking at me with a hopeful look in his eye. One that made it impossible to turn down. Maybe he wasn't a creep. Maybe he did do all this charitable acts of kindness to all foreigners.

Maybe my dad wouldn't mind coming home a little later than usual. After all, it wasn't like as if he cared. But then again...

"I have homework." I blurted out, and instantly regretted my words when I saw his face fall for a minute.

"I'm sure they didn't leave you with a lot of homework, after all its only your first day of school. And plus, your dad wouldn't mind having a cop guide you. He'd actually be thrilled that his son would be safe. Come on, let's walk to a park that I know of around here i'd think you might like it." No, kidding I scoffed inwardly. I've been feeling a little on the edge ever since this cop has come around being all friendly. At the first meeting it was fine... but now, isn't it a little too much?

I slowly moved my body to walk with him and as we did, Raizo pointed out the tall buildings with extraordinary light displays. He said that at night the city would be all lit up and anyone could get their hands on the best street food around. He said that the city would get so dark, that there would be no stars in the sky, and it was sad to him because he loved seeing the sky. He told me to get away from the busy city life he would go into the forest and look at the moon and stars.

"Aren't you scared of being alone in the dark? Where there's nobody around?" I arched my brow at him.

"What? Are you worried about me already? We just meet..." He teased and I couldn't help but let the feeling of embarrassment wash over me as I let the feeling sink in. Of course he wouldn't be afraid, he's a cop and a guy who had big muscles on him. A short and skinny guy like me would probably be afraid if I didn't have anyone around.

"Yeah..." I chuckled awkwardly.

"You should come with me one night." He said making me stop in my tracks.

"T-to go camping of course! You can even bring Hajime along if you'd like." He mumbled under his breath. He sounded as if he didn't mean that though.

"I'll think about it. But won't you be busy and all, being a cop, and rescuing the city from bad citizens?"

"Nah, Japan has been kind and peaceful lately... I don't think there would be any dangers any time soon." He said with a smile.

"Look, we're here already." He said as he guided me to the most beautiful park that i've ever seen. It was all lush green and we walked through a pathway on either side of us were tall pink flowered trees. They were the most beautiful trees that I've ever seen!

"They're cherry blossom trees." He told me. How did he know what I was going to ask? "They're beautiful aren't they?" He smiled as I stared at them gawkingly."T-they are..." I breathed out a cloud air as I looked through each tree.

When we came across a bench we decided to eventually sit down and take a seat. It was oddly really relaxing but the states that we were getting were making me uncomfortable.

Otousan would glare at them every time they did that.

"Why do they stare at me like that?"

"You're a foreigner. We don't see them often here." He explained."So tell me about yourself."

"There's not much to tell. I moved here because of my dad's job and my mom died when I was little." I shrugged my shoulders."Can I ask you something?" I hesitantly asked him.

"Anything..."

"Why do you want me to call you daddy?"A surprised look washed over his face as he refused to meet my gaze. Here goes nothing.

Red Flags

Maybe I shouldn't have said anything.

I mean, what was supposed to be a relaxing time now turned to be a hot mess. And it was because of my stupid mouth. It always got me into trouble. Did I really want to know why he wanted me to call him daddy? Yes, ok maybe not. It honestly scared me the cop in front of me looked like a dear caught in headlights.

"Where did you get that idea from?" Tanaka asked.

"Google translate." I blurted out.

When in reality, I got that from Hajime. But I was too shy to admit it. I couldn't help but feel a little proud at that. But Tanaka for some reason wasn't, he frowned and he looked like he was going to laugh any second now. Did I just make myself look like a dumb white boy?

Whatever, anything to make this awkwardness seem less awkward.

"I used to go there all the time to write my Spanish essays. I'd write them in English first then copy and paste them to google translate." Tanaka barked out a hearty laugh as he slapped his knee cap. I don't get it did I say something funny? I was trying to be serious.

"Hate to break it you Lark-kun, but google translates aren't 100% accurate. How did your essays turn out?" He smiled.

"Well...I guess that would explain the C's and sometimes D's I would get on my papers." I muttered awkwardly while rubbing neck.

"You're so cute." Tanaka whispered making me involuntarily blush. What guy calls another guy cute? I'm a boy, I prefer hot, sexy, or like my granny calls me a handsome young man. But not cute, cute is for girls or fluffy cats. It's degrading.

"I have balls not a vagina cute is for girls." I scoffed. "Believe me I know that." He mused while giving me a once over. Wait what? Now we're going off topic here! I see what he's trying to do he's trying to manipulate my innocent mind by trying to have things his way. But no, that's where I put my foot down. "Don't try to change the subject!" I said making him raise his eyebrows when I said that louder than I needed to. OhShit, I think I peed a little when his eyes glared down slightly they also looked a shade darker than they were. His shoulders squared but he looked like he was trying to shake off my outburst. He rolled his neck around and his eyes were softer this time, it was weird really. I gulped, trying to fight this weird feeling to say that I was sorry. There was just something about him, that made me want to tuck my tail between my legs and apologize.

"S-sorry." I mumbled, making him arch a brow his frown turned into a small smile.

"Its alright. But in the future, i'd like you to restrain from raising your tone when you're talking to me." What? I shot my eyes up at him in alarm. The hell? He noticed my expression and said "I mean after all, in Japan its a custom to not disrespect your elders. You speak to authority or those who are older than you with respect." He crossed his bulging arms over his chest and puffed it out proudly.

"Right, I didn't know that." I muttered, feeling bad that I opened my big mouth.

"Its no matter, Lark-kun, it's not your fault that you don't know our customs. But to answer your question from before otousan does not mean Daddy, it uh means.... respectable elder."

"Oh." That's weird, than why did Hajime said it meant daddy? Hajime is young and still learning English. Maybe he didn't now what that really meant. I'll let it slide for now then, now that Raizo told me what it mean.

"Okay then." I said with a smile, making him in turn smile back. Besides, it wouldn't be reasonable for a cop to want someone to call him that anyways.

There was another awkward silence when a small ice cream truck came passing by ringing his bell. My mouth started drooling but I fought against it. I couldn't have any more sweets. Raizo called the ice cream man over with a wave of his hand. The two of them started saying something in Japanese something that I didn't understand.

Man, I really should pick up some lessons at the academy. And maybe learn the Japanese currency too that might help. Raizo and the ice cream man exchanged money and two sorbets. Yum. He must be really hungry to eat those two on his own. Like the greedy person I Sam I couldn't help but eye the sorbet.

Raizo said his goodbyes to the ice cream man and held out the two sorbets in front of me. Making my eyes widen in shock. "No, no, no I couldn't... .you've already done so much for me already."

"One of them is yours I figured you'd like the fruity flavored one instead of green tea." He mused, making me frown. Why does everyone have a way to make me feel like I'm five? "A-re you sure?" I asked, still eyeing the pink sorbet.

"Please do."Before he could change his mind and keep it for himself I took the ice cream off his hands."Thanks." I blushed knowing that I took it away too quickly. Maybe I shouldn't have done that, it was too late to change his mind anyways but it looked like he didn't care. We ate our cones in a comfortable silence. And even though I hoped that he wouldn't notice, I couldn't help but secretly admire his strong and handsome features. Wait...what am I thinking? I can't think that way about a guy... i'm not gay. Just because I appreciate another guys looks doesn't mean that i'm not gay. What's wrong with me? I looked like the cop was going to say something again but I couldn't help but notice that the sun was about to set.

Shit, double shit. I really had to go home, my dad set up a curfew for me. I gobbled down my ice cream in one go, not caring that my brain instantly had a brain freeze. I clasped the side of my head with my left hand and winced.

"Hey not so fast there...you don't want to get a tummy ache eating that so quickly."

I looked up at him a little annoyed. Really? How old does he think I am? Five?

"I had a great time today Tanaka but it looks like its getting late, and I have to go home." I muttered regrettably under my breath. I scurried around and swooped up my backpack from underneath the bench and stood up. Tanaka stood up at the same time and almost looked disappointed? That's weird. "Oh...I you're right. I guess I held up your time, sorry about that." He said with a flushed expression on his face while rubbing the nape of his neck with his opposite hand. "I got to get going. Thanks for everything, really." I said while trying to brush past him, I couldn't help but jump a little though when his hand grasped onto my wrist. I looked past him over my shoulder with an arched brow. What did the cop want this time? He's already done and offered more than enough for me, and now i'm beginning to think that its really getting suspicious.

Tanaka-san held onto my wrist, "maybe I can offer you a ride home. Surely your dad would be wondering why you're home so late, and I can lend you a hand on that." He said with a grin. It was true, my dad would be wondering why I was so late. But I was a little peeved at the face that he was trying to offer me another ride home. I read somewhere online once, that you couldn't trust strangers that you didn't know in a foreign country. All sorts of strange things could happen. But this guy was a cop, what could possibly go wrong? I gulped, as I tried to come up my decision.

"I-I guess. Sure why not?" I chuckled nervously, tugging my hand out of his grip. His smile widened creepily. He almost looked a bit too thrilled that I accepted his offer, wouldn't most cops be annoyed with helping out a dumb foreigner like me?

"Come along then." He sang as he walked by my side down the path way of the cherry blossom trees. As we got to the side walk to where his car was parked I couldn't help but frown and notice that there was so much traffic and it was only 6 o'clock. Japan's traffic was twice the size of the traffic in Sacramento maybe even L.A. The city that was known to have the most traffic....my dad was going to kill me. As I got into his passenger's side of the car I began to tap my feet anxiously and started counting off the seconds then the minutes as to how long the drive would take. The cop changed lanes but it felt like we weren't moving at all. I was starting to think that he purposely took the long way back to my home because even though it was only 25 minutes on the road it felt like an eternity.

Its been an hour and we were hardly moving. Was this his plan all along? Why did a cop suddenly take so much interest in me as to go all his way to help a foreign guy like me? A loud buzz began to vibrate against my pants making me jump out of my train of thoughts. I reached into the front pocket of my jeans and took out my flip phone and saw that my dad was calling. Crap, I had 5 missed calls from him I was really late and he is going to be so pissed at me. I gulped and hesitated on whether or not I should ignore his call.

"Are you going to answer that? Its your phone..." Tanaka mused as he tried to glance over and see my collar ID, but I moved it away before he could.

"Its my dad he's going to kill me. I'm so late...." I moaned, I jumped again when I heard what appeared to be a low growl from his throat? Was he growling? Can humans actually do that? Or was I just hearing things. Tanaka cleared his throat.

"No one is going to die on my watch." He assured me, when all of a sudden the lights on his police mobile went blaring off as cars started to move out of their way so that he could pass. You've got to be kidding me, he could have done this the whole time? I knew he was doing it on purpose. As the cars parted their way, he easily sped through the highway past the red stoplights and what was supposed to be an hour more drive turned out to be a 28 minute drive back to my house. I breathed a huge sigh of relief when we passed the flickering lamppost that flickered on and off annoyingly. Tanaka noticed that lamppost too, "you really should get that fixed you can't see very well at night with that."

"I know." I muttered, gulping as waves of nerves racked through me when I saw my dad's angry face in front of my house. It looked like he got even angrier when he saw that I was inside a cop car. But could I blame him? I would be scared shitless too if I saw my own son come back home late in a cop car, in a foreign country while it was dark outside. I gulped as I shrank into my seat as Tanaka parked and turned off the lights.

"Don't worry Lark, i'm going to make sure nothing happens to you." Thanks, but my dad could be a really mean and intimidating guy when he wanted to be. Tanaka was the first to step out of the car and he tried to smile and be nice but my dad brushed it off.

"What did he do this time!?" He yelled before turning to me pointedly making me shrink under his harsh glare. I was so glad that these windows were dark so that he couldn't see me on the other side.

"Get out of that car boy!" He barked, making me wince as I hesitantly and ever so slowly opened my side of the car door. Tanaka stood in front of me as my dad tried to look at me but it looked like the cop wasn't having any of my dad's attitude.

"Sir, please calm down and allow me to explain why your son was late." He was doing that weird throaty growl thing. Dad's form was shaking as he took a few sniffs in the air and a tick formed in his jaw.

"You don't need to explain anything....I want you to stay away from my son from now on Tanaka Raizo. You and the rest of your kind!" What was going on here? Tanaka's shoulder's were shaking as he tried to fight for his self control. "That's not really polite there sir, I have just giving your son a ride home and taken him a tour of the city. Your son did nothing wrong believe me, if you would like to blame anyone blame me. I'm the one at fault, I was the one who brought him home late."

I stepped around Tanaka's frame "Dad?" I asked unsurely his suddenly dark eyes flashed to me and he grabbed me by the arm and pulled me close to him. "Thank you for your hospitality but it is no longer needed. Thank you." He said while forcing me to turn around and dragging me back into the house. I looked back and noticed Tanaka's worried face and I tried to show him that I was going to be fine but he didn't look so convinced by it. My dad opened the door got us inside and slammed it shut making me wince. He looked towards me and frowned with his arms across his chest.

"I don't want to see you around that man ever again son, is that understood?"

"Why? What was so bad about him, he was just showing me around dad." I fought back.

He rolled his eyes. "Look, I know I haven't been around much ever since your mother died but i'm here now alright and i'm telling you that he's not somebody you want to be around. Not even his friends okay? Stay away from him and his cult. I didn't hear great things about that cop or the people that he hangs out with at work okay?"

"But dad!"

"Listen to me for once in your life!" He snapped. "Stay away from that man and his cult worshiping buddies, just go to school and come straight back home alright?" He snapped. Not wanting to anger him anymore than he was I nodded my head. How can a cop that treated me so nicely be something that made my dad so scared? My dad was hardly the type of man to be scared of anything or anybody. What made Tanaka Raizo so different?

"Sure dad." He sighed a breath of relief and ran a hand through his hair already looking tired. I felt bad for wearing him out.

"There's pizza on the counter top, eat it before it gets cold. I'm going to bed." He muttered as he brushed past me.

"Aren't you going to have some?" I asked awkwardly despite the fact that we were shouting at each other minutes ago. He shook his head and just walked up the steps leaving me alone to my dinner I sighed and sat down at a lone chair. Its always been like this with me and him....ever since mom died, we've never been close it was frustrating. I guess I could just have a few slices of pizza and start on a little bit of homework. I looked down hoping to find my back pack but paled a bit when I suddenly remembered that I left my back pack back in the cop's car! I slammed my head down on the table a couple of times.

So much for staying away from Tanaka Raizo.

A/N: Hello! If you're enjoying The Hunt please check out my new story Escaping a Possessive Vampire...its a m/f story and I hope you give it a chance. Let me know what you think! Love you all! XD

~~~~~~~~~~

"You will never leave me, you will be mine for all eternity."

Vampires, werewolves and all supernatural creatures are tired of hiding, and now roam freely in society, in an every day high lifestyle while the humans live in poverty. Vampire control society, while the humans are at the bottom of the food chain, again. But in order to co-exist peacefully with the humans all eligible male and female donors from 16-21 years of age must be drafted for the Selection. If chosen for the Selection one lucky male or female would receive 60% of rations to support their families for the entire year in exchange for their blood. The only rule is, that neither the donor nor the blood recipient can fall in love with each other.

To some families, being a blood donor brings them hope out of poverty, but to one human...it means anything else but hope.
~~~~~~~~~~

Ditch Day

"**Y**ou remember what I told you last night, don't you son?"

My dad asked me furrowing his eyebrows, almost like he was warning me, challenging me. It was an awkward morning, as we were trying to eat breakfast as calmly possible. I really wanted to ask him though, why doesn't he like Tanaka Raizo? What was so bad about him that got him riled up?

"Son, I asked you a question and I expect an answer." He said while crossing his strong looking arms in a threatening way. I gulped and nodded my head slowly.

"Y-yes sir." Maybe its too late to mention to him that I left my backpack in the back of his car. I don't think he would be too happy for him to hear that. How was I going to get that back if he wanted me to stay away from him so badly, I bit my tongue in retaliation at the thought of it. I didn't want to start something that I knew I was going to regret later.

"Good." He said while crossing one long leg over the other and spreading out the morning newspaper before him. As I looked more closely at it, I noticed it was in Japanese, everything was. I couldn't watch T.V. anymore because I could barely understand what they were saying. I should pay attention to my Japanese class more often and practice that whenever I could get the chance to. It might come in handy after all.

"Dad? How'd you come to learn Japanese?" My dad hummed as the strong scent of coffee wafted through the air he reached his arm out and took a long zip before pointedly looking at me.

"School, when I was in college I took three years of it as an elective, and then began to apply it in daily life. I can't tell you how many times I see my colleagues taking Japanese or any kind of foreign language only to never be able to pick it up and learn it fluently. Pathetic really." He tsked, ouch, that wasn't very friendly.

"Why do you ask? Do you want to learn?" He asked with an arched brow. "Yeah, I kinda do, but I suck at it." I scoffed while he smirked and arched a brow in a playful way.

"Learning a new language is hard but not impossible to do. You should pursue it in your studies at the academy, take advantage of practicing it now that we're in Japan. You should practice it with the locals anybody really except with Tanaka Raizo." He said sternly.

"Y-yeah, I won't forget that part." I promised half-heartedly. I try to stay away from him, but somehow always finds his way back to me, its weird, I'll get over that though. "Dad? Can I ask you something?"

"Sure...anything, shoot."

"What kind of job do you do here in Japan? You never told me about it." I said while looking absent mindly at my cereal and spinning the spoon around the milk.

"I can't really tell you that right now....one day though I will." He said with a smile while looking at the watch on his wrist. "Shouldn't you be on your way to school right now?"

"Shit!" I cried out while pushing the chair out of the way as I stood up. "I'm late for school."

"Language son."

I ran out the door trying to take in as much of my cereal as possible while grabbing a granola bar on the go.

"See ya' later dad!" I called out to him, while grabbing my uniform jacket and putting on. I slammed the door shut behind me and started running to the campus, even without my backpack. I hoped my dad didn't notice that I had that missing. The academy was 10-15 minutes away from my house, conveniently. And I couldn't help the hope that rose within' me, I could probably make it on time if I speed it up. I passed by corridors, cherry blossom trees, and I even hit some people on my to the academy. I tried telling them that I was sorry, but I don't think anybody understood that. I brushed it off though, and couldn't help the small smile on my face when I finally saw the gates to my school. I was going to make it! I thought, as I pumped my arms to my side, my hair blowing in the wind, as my heartbeat accelerated.

I just had to!

My heartbeat was pounding so loudly that I could have sworn I could hear it in my ears. Just a few more minutes and I can make it past those gates. My eyes widened, however, when I saw the campus guard approaching the gates from behind, almost like he was ready to lock them in place.

No!

No, no, no, noooo! I screamed in my head.

"Wait!" I cried out to him while holding my hand out to him. The guard smirked while looking at me, and then pointing at his watch signaling that I was late. I forgot the policy that they had that the school closes its front gates at a certain time. He pulled out his keys and started to whistle as I felt my lungs beginning to burst from running so much. Sweat was forming around the temples of my forehead, and my breathing was beginning to turn ragged.

He closed the gates while laughing and turning away.

"Fuck!" I cried out, as I finally approached the gates. I let out a dry heaving wheeze while bending over and putting my hands on my legs, trying to catch my breath. I grabbed onto the metal bars and began to shake them, trying to grab the guard's attention.

"Hey! Hey, mister you can't do this to me! Please! I'm a transfer student! I'm new here!" I cried out while slamming the gates repeatedly. You'd think they care? No. The guard pretended to ignore me and walked away in a mocking gesture. I couldn't help but gaze at his retreating figure in defeat, as I slid down onto the floor with my back against the gates. "Damn..." I whispered. Now what was I going to do? I looked around the brick walls, hoping that I can climb my way in but that wasn't going to work. At the top of the walls, the bricks had the barbed circle like wires. Even if I could try to get over them, it wouldn't help me anyway. My dad was going to kill me, now how was I going to be able to get into the school without being caught?

I could call my new friend that I made, but I didn't have his number to do it. A thought suddenly hit me, maybe I could just skip school. After all, I did leave my backpack in Tanaka's car. For once that seemed like the best option to do.

Or so I thought...A familiar sound of car pulled up around the school and I froze when it seemed that it pulled up in front of...me? I slowly turned around to see a familiar police car, and inside of it was Tanaka Raizo. The devil himself, so much for trying to stay away from him. I thought as I started shuffling between my feet uncomfortably. Tanaka walked out of the driver's seat and pulled out a familiar looking bag.

My back pack! He still has it! I gulped as he smiled and walked towards me with my school bag.

"Tanka!" I cried out shakily and tried to smile at him but my smile was wobbly. "What are you doing here?" I cocked my head to side curiously, even though it was obvious why he was here.

"You forgot your backpack in my car the other night, and I thought that well since you couldn't have a successful school day without all your necessary utensils I thought i'd just drop it off for you instead." He said with a smile as he stood a good distance away from me while handing my backpack out towards me. I graciously took it and strapped around my shoulders onto my back so that it was a nice fit.

"Thank you, I don't know what to say, it was a nice surprise for you to come all this way."

"It was nothing, really....but if I may be so bold in asking, why aren't you inside of the academy?" Tanaka asked with an arched brow.

"Uhmmm...I was locked out 'cause I was late." I replied pathetically, hanging my head in defeat.

Tanka let out a barking laugh while throwing his head back at my lame answer. "You must have forgotten that Japanese schools are different from American schools." He said with a smile as I shrugged my shoulders.

"You wouldn't happen to be able to let me inside would ya'?" I asked hesitantly, even though I knew I was pushing my limits here with this generous cop.

"You know I can't do that as much I would like to help you. The academies here take their rules very seriously unfortunately."

"I see." Guess I'll just have to ditch school then.

"I would offer you a ride back to you house but you dad wouldn't be very fond of that idea."

"No, he wouldn't."

"Lark...do you have anything planned for today? Maybe I could treat you to something at the coffee shop seeing as its still early in the morning." I thought about his answer, and shrugged my shoulders ruefully. What did I have to lose? My dad was already at work.

"Sure." I said as we mirrored each others smiles.

I had some questions to ask him, and I wasn't going to take no for an answer.

Questions

"So, where are we going?" I asked Tanaka as we got into his police car. I never thought I'd be in this situation in one in my life, being inside of a police car that is. But there's a first time for everything I guess.

"Its still morning I think we could start off by grabbing some breakfast, assuming that you're late for school you missed it right?" I couldn't fight the deep blush that rose on my cheeks.

"Oh Lark, you can't miss breakfast its the most important meal of the day." Tanaka chided while wagging his finger back and forth in a condescending way.

"Yeah...I had to give that a rain check this morning." I admitted making him laugh while starting the engine of his car, he put in reverse, rolled out of the parking space he was in and took off. To be honest, breakfast grosses me out. I normally skip out on it and i'm fine eating lunch and dinner on my own. As we were driving through the busy street life of Sapparo, I gazed out the window and couldn't help but be left awe struck by the scenery. I was definitely not in America, everything was so different here compared to my home. I couldn't help but feel nervous on what my dad's going to think now that I missed the second day of school. It didn't look good on my civil record or on my academic one.

My leg started bopping up and down as nerves started spicking up in me.

At least, I had my backpack back though. I thought to myself with a scoff, I couldn't help but jump a little though when I felt a warm hand touch my knee. My leg stilled almost immediately at the contact. My eyes darted down to the hand on it and up to Tanaka who's eyes were still focused on the road. He must have put his hand there by mistake, I realized with a gulp. He'll take it off eventually. After about a minute or two of me looking at his eye to him just humming I put two and two together that he wasn't going to take that hand off.

I decided, to distract myself from the hand on my leg, I gazed out on the window and soaked everything in. It was a cloudy morning, and everywhere I looked the streets were filled with people and there was no arm length between them. It was twice the size of little ole' San Fransisco. Filled with street lights and advertisements everywhere you looked and foreign letters. I don't know how I was going to get used to living here in Japan. I barely made a friend a few days ago, and my dad is always off on work duty leaving me alone at home. Maybe it was a good thing to have a cop as a friend in a foreign country it could come in handy after all. My eyes strayed away from the window and I looked over to Tanaka who was humming to himself as he was driving. "So...where are we going?" I asked hesitantly, maybe it wasn't a good idea to trust Tanaka so easily. After all, he was still a stranger to me. We hardly knew anything about each other and we only just met a few days ago. No wonder my dad was so mad at me for hanging out with a cop. No wonder he had his doubts around this man. I still find it a little odd how he still wanted to get to know me more but I was literally half his age. What kind of cop would still want to hang out with someone who's my age?

"Are you alright there Lark-kun? You've been awfully quiet..." Yeah, of course i'm quiet i'm trying to figure out wether or not you re actually trying to kidnap me or not. I've just given you the opportunity to. Why do I trust him enough to not run away? "I-Its n-nothing, don't worry about it." I said reassuringly. "If you say so." Tanaka chuckled and instead of dropping his hand on my knee he gave it a gentle squeeze. I still didn't say anything about the hand and looked straight ahead as I felt my heart beat quicken.

"Looks like we're going to be on the road for a while Lark-kun, there's a lot of traffic today. And its unusual because its early in the morning..." He hummed as he started giving my knee a small massage. I put my chin in my hand and arched a brow at that as we continued to be in an awkward silence for a little longer. His hand that was on my knee was slowly rising up to my thigh until his hand stopped a few inches from my no no zone. I let out a low gasp, hoping he wouldn't hear it. His hand was too far up was he gay? Why was he ouching me like that? I really hoped that he wasn't going to do what I think he was going to do.

I gulped when he gave my thigh another firm squeeze, I looked at him from the corner of my eye but he was still looking at the road ahead as if nothing is really happening. What was up with this creep? Can you really blame me for not freaking out about his hand? He was a man more than half my age, was he a pedo? "Just out of curiosity Lark...how old are you?" I gulped a little, my throat suddenly feeling as dry as cotton. Should I answer that?

"16." I was really dumb wasn't I?

"Oh, I see..." Tanaka almost looked disappointed when I revealed my age to him, and once I told him he dropped his hand from my leg making me let out a breath of relief. "Looks like we're at the cafe." He said with a smile as he perfectly parrallel parked in between a tight space. A car was in front of him and another car was behind him and I couldn't help but lean over my shoulder and look back at the front just to make sure he wasn't going to hit any of the cars. But he didn't miss, not even once!

And they said that Asians couldn't drive or see.

I felt a small smirk creep onto my face at the thought but brushed it off when he put the gear into park and unbuckled his seat belt. "Come on then Lark, breakfast is calling." When I slowly reached over and was about to click my seatbelt open Tanaka stopped me and did it for me.I arched a brow at that as he looked up at me with a soft but knowing smile....okay. That was not weird at all, I thought to myself. Before getting out of the police car I was careful to make sure that the car door didn't swing open and hit anything on my way out. I slowly stepped out and made my way around the police car and to his side.

"I've never been inside of a police car before." I told him making him smile. "Did you like it? It doesn't have to be the first time you'll ride in it."

I laughed awkwardly. Not daring to question that as we made our way towards a small cafe that had cats on top of it and cats inside of it. Cats?

"Are you fond of cats Lark?"

"Yeah...I think. I like dogs more though." I told him honestly, not wanting to hurt his feelings by bringing me here. Honestly, i've never been around a cat long enough to actually like one. I've only grown up with dogs in my life.

"Where are we exactly?" I looked at the entry sign to the unusual cafe but I couldn't translate to what it said in English. All I knew was that there was so many cats inside of a cafe, is that legal?

Tanaka opened the door for me and let me go before him, making me feel like more than a girl already. Geezzz....I fought the rising blush that threatened to surface and walked inside careful to avoid bumping into him or making any physical contact with him. The moment I walked in I l heard the loud sounds and screeches of meows and saw that we were the only two guys here, great.

"Welcome to Sapporo cat cafe! Home to homeless kitties waiting for you to take home and be with their new families. Did you know? That cats are sadly one of the most abandoned and abused animals here in Japan? It is our job to rescue these kitties and make sure that they're placed in loving homes." Is it just me or did that sound like she was memorizing a script? I may not be fond of cats, but I did feel sad to hear that story.

"Thank you, we would like to meet a few cats and order a few drinks." Tanaka answered. The girl turned towards him and blushed a little, making a silver of jealousy flare up in me. Wait jealous? I shook my head.

"O-of course officer! But unfortunately there is a fee to pay if you want to meet the cats, each payment makes sure that cats are well fed and have what they need. We pay by the hour." She said with a smile making him nod as he looked at the watch on his wrist. Now that i've noticed it, I looked around the room and saw that all the Japanese women were eye raping Tanaka-san.

"Yes of course where do I pay?" He asked getting his wallet out of his pocket.

"Right over here!" The short Japanese girl chirped as she led him over to an isolated office desk. I stood there awkwardly, not knowing what else to do with my time as my eyes peered through the glass door that had a lot of cats in it. Its been several minutes since i've stood there waiting for Tanaka until he arrived with a big smile on his face and a set of keys. "Ready?"

Do I have a choice?

The Japanese girl from before came back with another annoying smile on her face. "My name is Kyoko and here is the locker room, if you open yours up inside you'll find a pair of slippers that you must put on in order to make your stay more comfortable. You can put your shoes inside the locker as well." Tanaka did as she said, and took out a couple of slippers for me first and started changing his shoes into his own pair as I did the same.

"Its not every day that we see a cop and a foreigner coming to one of our cafes. What part of America are you from?" Kyoko asked while looking at me.

I swallowed the lump in my throat, i've never been good at small talk. Its part of my anxiety. "San Fransisco."

"Ah, very nice." She said fakely.

"Well, here you are...enjoy you're time remember when the time is up please return your keys and slippers to us thank you for saving a cat today. If you find that some cats are less affectionate than others you can always try to draw them with treats however those will cost extra as well."

Damn, everything was so expensive in Japan.

"Enjoy your time, i'll bring your drinks shortly." She said while closing the door behind her softly. Did she ever shut up?

"You didn't have to buy me any drinks Tanaka, but thanks anyways." Tanaka flashed me a smile. "It was not a problem really I figured it would give us some time to talk about some things and clear the air."

"Yeah, I think that would be necessary..." I said to him as we sat down in a corner with an open window. It was quite for awhile until a small cute cat jumped into my lap taking me by surprise. My eyes widened and my hands were up in a mock surrender.

"Ah, its a Siamese cat." Tanaka chuckled as he started stroking her furr. She was such a friendly thing. I couldn't help but smile and instantly feel relaxed by petting her. I almost felt a growing attatchment to her.

"Hey girl, what's your name?" I asked softly feeling an overwhelming sense of protection that I can only point out as motherly.

Tanaka reached for her collar, "her name is Gigi." He smiled. "She seems to like you." I couldn't help but smile at that and felt a swell of pride rise in my chest as I stroked her fur. She stretched her front paws on my pant leg and let out a cute yawn meow, showing off her teeth. I laughed at that and began to stroke her ears and let the wave of peace overflow me.

"Lark, we really do need to discuss somethings." I instantly stopped petting the cat and felt the smile turn into a frown.

"Okay then, lets talk."

Here goes nothing.

Daddy Issues

I'm not stupid, nor am I an idiot either. Wait, are those two the same thing?

Either way, I knew what he was trying to do. He's trying to distract me from figuring out the one thing I wanted to know the most. "I'm not an idiot." Tanaka raised an amused brow at me, great he was mocking me already. "I know you're not Lark-kun, I've never said you were in the first place." He hummed.

"I'm not an idiot, but why are you trying so hard to spend time with me for? Don't you have other things to do as a cop?" I didn't want to sound rude at this point, but I was still on the edge. Come on, if you were in my shoes wouldn't you be creeped out if an oddly attractive Japanese policeman was so desperate to spend some time with you? When he could be clearly doing something else? I could have easily walked back home and watched some anime on my labtop or go on pornhub or something valuable to do with my time. "Pardon me if I seemed to offend you Lark. But, you do seem to sound oddly offended by some reason? Did I do something wrong?" He was trying to be cheeky with me. I narrowed my eyes at him, there was no way absolutely no way that I was letting him turn the tables on me! I'm trying to get answers here. Something is not normal about our relat---or friendship.

"I know for one thing that you lied to me." I said bluntly while staring at him directly in the eyes. I didn't care that we were in public for that matter, I wanted answers and now.

"Lied to you? What do you mean?"

"I know that otousan really means daddy. And not respectable elder or some bullshit like that. I've looked it up myself multiple times. Google really, and I've asked around. Why do you insist on me calling you daddy?" I pressed, pursing my lips together as I tried to coax it out of him, it was true though. I did do my research, and he did lie to me. But why? Should I be worried that he might be a pedo? I really didn't want to be a victim, but it looks like i'm putting myself at risk by spending some 'quality time' with him. I watched and waited for his reaction carefully, his body posture stiffened. His shoulders were squared and he squeezed his eyes shut while clenching his hand into a fist. I gulped, suddenly regretting my interrogation. The cat on my lap meowed and cocked his cute little head at the cop. Is it bad that I might use the cat as a shield in case things were about to go down? As if sensing my unease, the cop relaxed his posture and slowly opened his eyes and I was confused when his lips curled into a smile.

"Yes, you're right." What!? I'm right? Yes! If I could I'd throw a fist bump in the air right now I totally would, but for the moment I just did it mentally.

"That does mean daddy, i'm sorry that I tried to convince you otherwise. But, I really would like it if you did call me that though."

Wait, rewind and freeze. Did I just hear that correctly?

"What?" I blurted out dumbly.

"Why? You're not my dad, so why would I call you daddy?" I said, getting uncomfortable. This conversation just took a weird turn. I moved the cat carefully off my lap as I started getting ready if I needed to run out the store.

"This really wasn't the way that I was hoping it would go. I had a plan and everything." He mumbled the last part so quietly, that I didn't think I was supposed to catch it or not but I did. Okay, he was definitely a pedo! I should have listened to my dad and stayed away from him! My hands involuntarily started to shake, we were in public too. Of all places we could be in to talk about a situation like this. "A-are you talking about a sugar daddy?" I asked stupidly. Now I was just being stupid and he sighed while running a hand desperately through his hair.

"No, they are entirely two different things! I can assure you!" He insisted. As he took out a clipboard that was in his hand bag and flipped through the contents of it. Once he found what he was looking for he looked around the room and his eyes landed on the lone two females who were far away from us. I looked at him first then towards them and back at him again. Was he expecting them to be able to hear what he has to say? Probably.

He leaned down and urged me to lean in as well. "Its more of a daddy/little boy relationship. "Daddy", and "little boy," though this half of the relationship hasn't received as much attention.This kind of submissive enjoys being treated like a child by his lover, most commonly calling his partner "daddy" both in and out of the bedroom. He's fully integrated with her inner child, not play-acting the character of a young boy in his relationship. And don't get me wrong, there is no role play scenario for the 'little boy' at all. For a submissive, being a child feels entirely natural, authentic and effortless whereas playing the role of a "grown-up" feels conversely like a forced and falsified act." He tried to explain to me.

"Kind of like BDSM" He shook his head. "Believe it or not, it started in BDSM. But unlike them, we establish limits, time of duration and conditions for mutual benefits. I would only be a mediatory mean for this." I blink at this, confused. My headache killing me from all the information being thrown at me at once.

"Unlike a daddy, a sugar relationship involves a sugar daddy namely an older and rich man willing to pay for you company be it with gifts personal well-being or cash. But seeing as you will be the little boy in the relationship you two will be offering me certain favors. That's one thing that you can say that is similar to a sugar daddy." He said.

"Favors?" I ask harshly. Not liking where this was heading. "Yes, but of course they will be mutual." He handed something to me then, a couple of pieces of paper but on the very top of it my eyes widened even more. It literally said Daddy/lb Contract on top of it. My eyes were practically bulging out of their sockets at this point. Is this really my life right now? "I-I now this is sudden Lark, but I really would like it you would consider it." He pursed as I scanned my eyes down the first set of rules on the contract. It read...

Daddy/little boy Rules and Obligations:

Rule #1: Always tell Daddy good morning and good night when you wake up and fall asleep. Daddy always wants to be the first thing you see in the morning and the last thing you hear at night.

Rule #2: Make your bed.

Rule #3: Make sure to eat breakfast, lunch and dinner every day. Daddy doesn't want his little boy to be starving himself or over-eating. Its important to be healthy mentally as it is physically.

Rule #4: Tell Daddy when you've had you're three meals a day.

Rule #5: Send pictures, and always text daddy and other cute things.

Rule #6: No phone after bedtime, put it on the other side of the room.

Rule #7: No self harm...

Rule #8: Tell Daddy if anything is bothering you, or if you couldn't follow a rule. If you couldn't follow a rule, the appropriate punishment is to be set in place. Although a naughty little boy can be sexy, its important to always follow the rules.

Rule #9: Daddy shouldn't have to remind you of the rules.

Rule #10: Do your best.

Rule #11: Remember that Daddy is very proud of you.

Rule #12: Always tell Daddy that you love him.

There was much more to the contract, like five more pages to be exact. And I couldn't help but blush at the last rule. "You don't have to agree with this right away, I'd like to give you some time to think this over. I pretty much threw this under the bus with you." He shrugged his shoulders, no shit.

"I don't know what to say." I really didn't.

"Don't say anything now, you may take the contract home with you and look it over of course there are some things that you may have to sign. And to keep things between us..." He said as he leaned forward making me unconciously lean back while keeping the contract close to my chest, hoping that no one around could take a peak at it.

"I would keep this conversation or our little meeting to ourselves Lark-kun." I gulped, I know what he meant by that.

He didn't want my father my real "daddy" to know.

Like an Animal

I t was very difficult to wait for his response.

I should have waited a little longer but the idiot in me didn't want to. Lark-kun in my eyes was too beautiful to resist. His beautiful brunette curls fanned over his face as his big brown eyes widened at the contract in his hands. I secretly wanted him to say yes right away but I knew that that was too rash, too irealistic to happen. And then, the worst did happen. Lark-kun gently pushed the cat to the side and I watched lamely as the cat meowed in protest trying to reach for him again.

"I-I'm sorry...Raizo but this is too new, too soon for me we hardly know each other." Lark-kun said softly at first while looking down. My heart sank, I honestly thought that he was the one I felt inside.

"Plus, I'm not..." He clicked his tongue with his teeth and looked at me with furrowed brows. "Into men." He said while looking at me in the eyes this time. My hands clenched into fists as I felt my jaw tighten and my body begin to shake. But I pushed it back, now wasn't the time. At least he had the decency to not shoot me down on the spot right away. But how was he not gay? He didn't push my hand away from his leg like most straight men do. When I was looking for partners before all of them pushed my hand away but he didn't! Unless...he was hiding from his father. He was scared of that poor excuse of a man...I felt my jaw tighten.

"Is it your father?" I pressed. He blinked and shook his head. "W-what?"

"Perhaps I didn't make myself clear, if so I apologize, but is it your father that is scaring you?" I pressed again.

"No!" He said quickly, all too quickly. I could hear his heart beat quicken and smell the fear that's coating his body. Something wasn't right with their relationship.

"But I'm not gay, I'm sorry Raizo. I'm not the guy you're looking for maybe they'll be someone else."

"No, there isn't someone else! There isn't going to be anybody else!" I wasn't surprised by my change of tone, and so was Lark-kun. I didn't want to scare him, and I couldn't afford to lose him. His blood was calling to me he had to be the one.

"The whole point of this trip Raizo! Is to find my brother!"

"I need to know why the shifters have taken him! And where?" Lark said in between short breaths before pausing and breathing.

"A-anyways, we can always be friends? Thanks for helping me around on my first few days of Japan. We can still hang out if you want?" He asked cutely while tilting his head to the side, he held the contract back to me, almost as if he expected me to take it back. " Keep it, in case you change your mind." I told him while standing up from the comfortable bench in the cafe, leaving my half cup of good coffee behind. My appetite was spoilt for the morning, I allowed my body to get closer to his and looked directly in his eyes. I grabbed his hands and smiled when i heard a small gasp escape his beautiful looking lips.

He will be mine.

I will have no other before him or after. His blood called to me, it was the rarest of them all.

Though I didn't tell him this, I caressed his fingers in mine and softly ran my thumb around him. "We will meet again Lark-Kun." I carefully watched his reaction and noted that if he really were a straight man, his cheeks wouldn't blush. He wouldn't let me hold his hands for this long, a straight man, from my experience would have pushed me away. Called me unfathomable names that I can not mention. And yet this beautiful boy did none of those things. I dared myself to lean forward so that I could whisper something to him.

"If you change your mind my number is in that contract. Though I am disappointed that you didn't agree, I know that I'll be the one to eventually change your mind." I let him go then, and frowned as I watch him scatter away from me and rush out of the cafe. I did have plans to follow him home to make sure that he was safe, but sadly that wasn't on the agenda anymore. He ran off before we even had the chance to finish our drinks. I sat back down feeling defeated for a moment until a familiar meow reached my ears. Gigi, the cat from before curled up against my legs and instantly started purring. Almost as if trying to comfort me in some way, I smiled and started stroking his furr. I didn't have any pets in my apartment, maybe I could adopt this friendly cat.

The lady from before came back in to check on everyone I assumed and when she glanced at me she smiled when she noticed the boy from earlier wasn't here. In the past, I've often had women claw on my feet begging me to take her in as her daddy because mostly everyone in the city knows who I am. They know what I do. But despite the many women and sometimes men that threw themselves at me, I ignored them. I wanted to wait for the right one, and the one that did come just seemed unattainable.

"Where is the American that was here with you?" She asked me in our native tongue.

"He left." I replied back to her solemnly, wishing nothing more than to be talking to Lark-kun right now instead of her. I took another sip of my drink, and stood up the moment she sat down next to me. She was one of them, I realized instantly how did I not notice it before? She must have mastered masking her scent when she's around dominants that she doesn't want. She's a sub. I could already smell her arousal around me, indicating that she was interested and I had to bite back the bile that tickled my throat.

"Is it true? That you're apart of the clan?" She asked with a slight purr in her voice.

"I'm wanton, and searching at the moment. If that boy wasn't interested earlier I could be a potential."

"No." I bit out at her. "He's the only one." I told her, as I took my leave from the cafe, I almost felt bad for leaving the cat with her but I had no space for a cat in my midst.

"I'm O negative!" She cried out desperately, making me freeze almost instantly as my blood started to throb and so did my canines. Almost everyone knew who I was, what I did and she just happened to pick up on it. I pushed my the rush back into my system unclouded the haze that just went through my vision and walked out the door. Satisfied to myself when I heard the chime of the bell, I resisted the call. I sighed to myself in relief. I resisted the blood lust. I heard ringing my ears, put my fist into my mouth and bit down on it hard. I slowly counted down from ten trying to get a hold of myself when I felt the vibrations of a cell phone in my pocket begin to ring.

I fished for the phone while keeping my hand in my mouth and flipped it open.

"What?" I snarled at the one who was at the other line.

"So....how did it go? Did he agree?" Satō Koichi chuckled at the other end of the phone.

"No." I bit out, making him laugh. "You really need to feed Raizo, the court won't be happy to hear that you're starving yourself to death. You're a valuable member to us, and you're job as a cop makes it easy for us to hide all the deaths that has been occuring around the city. Your job makes it easy for you to catch a feed. If Lark-kun is not wanton than get another who is! Even if its just for 5 minutes!" Koichi

"You don't understand Satō, I only want the boy, no one else." He tsked.

"Well, the boy doesn't want you. So why bother chasing him for? You need a potential until you can have the boy to yourself as not only a parter but to satisfy your blood lust. You're starving Raizo, if you don't feed within' the next 24 hours we will have to feed you a dead body by force."

I sighed, feeling angry and frustrated all at once. He was right though, I really did need to feed. The last i've eaten was in months, we normally have to supply ourselves once or at least twice every month to be stable. I hated feeding off of the humans, it made me feel more like an animal than a man. I normally feed off of animals but they're not enough...they don't give you the rush that a human's blood does.

"Alright..." I hissed at Koichi. "Remember Raizo, we will know if you haven't feed. If you don't feed, we will be forced to remove you."

"Fuck!" I cried out, while nearly smashing the phone in my hands. The citizens of Sapparo looked at me alarmed, probably not being used to seeing a cop swearing in public. I brushed it off though, and instantly thought back to the wanton girl in the cafe. She will have to do...despite the protest that rose within' in me, and the bile I felt...I had to feed. Or I will starve, I couldn't wai that much for Lark-kun. And by the time he knows everything I hope he will understand the choices I had to make to survive.I rushed back inside of the cafe to look for the wanton girl I saw her behind the cashier desk. And i've noticed that the hair that she held in a bun was now lose and long down her waist. As if sensing my presence she moved her hair over her shoulders, exposing her neck to me. Once again, I felt the blood rushing and pumping in my veins.

"Back so soon? What changed your mind?" I ignored her, grabbed her wrist and urged her to go into the back where no one would notice her missing. I pushed open the door to the back and slammed her to the wall making her gasp and her eyes sparkle. It almost disgusted me to see wanton humans willing to offer themselves so willingly to us. I pushed her shoulders back, leaned her neck to the side and listened very carefully for that delicious pulse. My mouth instantly began to sallivate at the thought of finally being able to feed even after so long. I allowed my canines to extend from their gums and without being gentle I pushed them into her veins. Letting the blood seep into me. The woman winced at first from the puncture of the skin, only to moan seconds later in pleasure, making me roll my eyes. It only took five minutes for me to drink when she started asking me to stop.

"Stop...please its too much. I feel faint."

The woman started to struggle beneath me but I held her rest tighter and tighter until she stopped struggling and fell limp in my arms. I started noticing that she was losing color and growing pale but I paid no mind to it as I finished the last drops and sucked her dry. Once done, I let her go, watching as she fell to the floor like a sack of potatoes. I noticed two puncture wounds on her neck, but they'll eventually fade. Like they all do...I made sure not to go in to deep because that would leave a scar, and it obvious questions. It probably wasn't smart of me, to have my feed during the day. Where all humans could possibly see but I was careful about it.

I turned away from the body in disgust as to what I have just done and reached for my phone to call Saitō, he picked up on the second ring.

"Its done, call the others to deal with the body. Get ready for the preparations."

"How does it feel to be back?" He asked cunningly making me roll my eyes. I didn't answer him, but instead decided to hang up. I hated what I was, I wasn't proud of it, but if I didn't drink I would die.

If I answered him back, though...

I would have said that it made me feel like an animal.

The Ramen Shop

I rushed out of that place as fast as I could without looking back. I still had the contract in my hands as I tried to push past the sea of people that were beginning to make me feel suffocated. I knew something was wrong with that man, the moment that he met me. I should have listened to my dad first and not meet up with him anymore! But what was I going to do? He always knew where I was, and where to find me. I was getting scared now. I felt unsafe to be around him. He wanted something out of me, what normal cop will be this close to a foreigner?

Much less a foreigner that he hardly knew to begin with! People were getting angry when I bumped into their shoulders but I really wanted to get away. I didn't want to be here right now, I wanted to go back home to the familiarity of San Fransisco! I suddenly stopped running, leaning over to bend and place my hands on my knees as I tried to catch my breath again.

I suddenly remembered that I still can't figure out how to get back home.

Fuck.

I pulled out my phone in the front of my pocket, ready to dial Hajime but then realized that he was also still in school. And I really didn't have his number. It was only the morning still...what was I going to do to kill some time? Go back to Tanaka? No way...I really was just going to go home and watch some Japanese T.V. or anime. I sighed impatiently as I walked much slowly now in a dazed and confused state.

What was I going do? I didn't think that by coming to Japan I'd already meet a possessive older gay man. I'm not gay, but why did he seem to think so? Was I giving him mixed signals? Maybe if I stay away from him for awhile he'll forget about me.

Yeah, right he will with the way he acted at the cat store. The noises of the city life and the busyness of it faded around me. As I looked at the contract in my hands. It weighed heavy as I touched it.

I decided to walk around the city, occasionally saying sorry to anybody that I've bumped into. And looked up when a huge screen TV was above me. It was my dad! I realized in shock, h-he was on T.V!

He was in the middle of an interview while speaking fluent Japanese. And I couldn't help but feel a swell of pride flood within me. A few of the locals have also started to gather around me and look at the screen.

"That's my dad." I told the person next to me. Knowing that they probably wouldn't understand crap of what I said.

But the funny thing is, that they did reply back with an annoyed glare? "Baka!" He just walked away. Whatever. I shrugged my shoulders but I've noticed as I looked up the screen one thing stood out. It looked like it was a company's name. And me being the brilliant guy I was. Put two and two together and deduced that that must be where my dad works. I heaved out a sigh of relief, and made sure to take a mental note of that. I had to find where my dad's job was so that he can send me back home. I still had trouble finding my way around the busy street life of Japan. And I hardly knew anyone except for Hajime and Tanaka. But I couldn't keep in contact with any of them. My best bet was to take a picture of the company's name with my phone and ask around with it.

I'm such a white boy.

As I was passing by people, I showed them a picture of the company's name and made flamboyant hand gestures trying to figure out if someone could tell me where it was. But they either just looked at me like I was stupid. Or they just brushed me off rudely and ignored me. Oh well. While walking around, i've noticed that I started getting hungry and that it was 11:30am. I normally have early lunch times, but I barely had any money on me. Crap. My stomach growled again, as I passed by a store that smelled of fresh ramen. I really wanted to go in and try some authentic ramen. Not that kind of instant noddle one that they sell at the dollar store but the real thing. I've noticed that the store was really popular, and I couldn't help but satisfy my curiosity and walked inside.

The store was filled with lively traditional Japanese music, and my nose was instantly hit with the smell of something salty. I didn't understand what everyone was saying around me, and I couldn't help but feel isolated. Isolated in a society, that i'm not comfortable with because I don't know the social norms. And I don't speak its language. Almost every table in the room was full and I found myself just standing there awkwardly. Being stunned in a room full of strangers. To my left, a group started laughing hysterically about something that I bet was funny. I wish I knew their language all of a sudden.

I rubbed my arm awkwardly, thinking of how stupid I am to walk in without any money. Shaking my head at myself, I was about to leave when someone caught my arm. Making me arch my brow as I turned around.

It was just a waitress.

"Eat-o, eat???" She asked me excitedly. Making me shake my head with a smile. "No dinero..."

I'm so stupid. This isn't Mexico.

"I mean, no money. I have nothing on me." I tried telling her, but she was insistent that I do eat. "Belly hungry." She pointed out with a smile. "You eat now, come come." She grabbed my hand without letting me have any excuses and dragged me off to an empty corner. She pulled out a menu on the table, and a few moments later came back with a glass of water and ice. She started preparing some grilled fish for me, separating the bones and splitting it in half. "While you wait on order, fish for you." She said with broken English. I nodded my head in thanks, as I tried to come up with a way to pay for the meal. Maybe if I didn't touch the food, she will get the hint that I have no way to pay for it. Suddenly, a group of loud people walked into the ramen shop. Yelling something in Japanese, that made everyone else shout back at them.

I smiled in confusion, trying to figure out what was going on. And then that's when I noticed they were white! Like me...As if one of them could read my mind she turned around and pointed in my direction. The guys around her noticed and walked towards me.

"Hey! Your American like us!" One of them cried out while slapping my shoulder and making me jump in surprise.

"Yeah, I guess."

"I'm Kyle, that dork over there is my sister Lane. And my two other friend, Dean and Sean." Sean nodded his head in acknowledgement towards me. But Dean just stayed quiet.

"What are you doing here in Japan for? Touring around, work?" Kyle asked, man was he nosy.

"Actually, its neither. My dad moved here recently and I'm going to that one academy for the foreigners."

"By God...so are we!" Lane cried out while clapping her hands excitedly, making Kyle snort. "Shut up Lane."

"This is one of the best ramen shops in Japan, did you know that?" He asked.

"No, honestly but I guess my nose must have because it smelled good." I told him bluntly making him frown a little. Sean started laughing and I was surprised to see even Dean start cracking up a smirk on that stoic face of his.

"Well, its good to know that at least your funny." Kyle said with a smile on his own. "So, where where you headed off to before stopping off at the ramen shop?" He asked nosily.

"I-I was actually lost, and couldn't find my way home. I was locked out of my school this morning, and I couldn't go back in but I stumbled into the shop but funny thing is I have no money on me." I chuckled, making everyone else laugh at the table.

"Wow, you just moved here?" He asked.

"Yeah, I did about three weeks ago."

"Three weeks, and a lot has already happened to you ain't it?" Kyle chided, making me nod my head in agreement. And that was when an idea hit me, maybe these guys knew about my dad's company and could take me there.

"Hey, i'm looking for my dad's company and I was wondering if you know where it is and you can probably show me where it is." I asked while reaching over my front pocket, pulling up the picture and showing it to him. He scratched his chin for a second and nodded, " heck yeah I do!

You're actually not that far away from it." He told me making me smile in relief. "Awesome."

"We can show you where it is, but...why didn't your dad just show you and tell him yourself?" Sean suddenly piped up.

"Yeah..." Lane but in, making me roll my eyes. "I honestly don't know, my dad just likes having his secrets I guess." I shrugged my shoulders making them mumble to themselves.

"Fair enough." Sean answered. "Hey, aren't you supposed to be in school today though its only 12 o'clock?" I asked them curiously making them all fall silent as their gazes went towards Dean. "Same reason you're." He muttered, making me shiver a little. There was something in his voice that was very deep and authoritative. It made me not want to question him and look away from him submissively. It was the strangest feeling I've ever got, stranger than meeting Tanaka. I noticed, however, that ever since they all sat here Dean couldn't stop staring at me. It was unnerving. It made Kyle chuckle, why was he laughing? "Don't mind Dean...he's just uh, always serious." Kyle laughed. Even as he laughed I still couldn't shake off that feeling of his eyes staring at me intently. It made me clench the paper in my hands even more tightly as I looked down on the fish.

Suddenly feeling that the fish was me.

Unsullied

I wanted to take back what I said. I didn't want things to be so awkward between us anymore. But how can that be, when we're still practically strangers.

Dean suddenly looked bigger than he already was, while the others seemed to look smaller. Did I say something I wasn't supposed to you? "What's your name again?" He asked. I blinked twice, surprised by how deep his voice sounded. There was something about him in general that was different than the others...so dominantly different.

"L-Lark." He arched a thick eyebrow, and leaned forward. "Last name? You look familiar." He said, why was it suddenly so hot in here? My heart started beating pretty fast now and my lips were getting dry. I licked my lips and nearly crushed the Daddy contract in my hands in order to stop them from shaking profusely. When I looked back up again his eyes seemed to grow darker when his eyes flickered down to my lips. Woah, what was that? What's happening right now?

"M-myers. Lark Myers."

"Shit." Dean cursed, and leaned back in his seat.

"Something the matter boss?" The whole room suddenly felt colder, and my skin started to feel like they have gotten chicken pocks.

"No," He bit back, but took one more look at me only softer this time. "Are you sure?" Lane asked with a mouthful of food.

"Laney! What did I tell you to do? Eat with your god damn mouth closed like a normal human for God's sake!" Seth barked out while slapping her back. Lane almost chocked on her food but swallowed it down anyways with huge gulps of water. My eyes widened at that, surprised by how her small body can eat so much. "Does she always eat like that?" I asked curiously while jabbing my thumb in her direction. Kyle started laughing, as the tension in the room suddenly lessened.

"You bet she does. I can tell you what else she can choke down too!" Kyle laughed again making some heads in around the room turn to our direction. Seth, however, looked really peeved that his sister was being made fun of. And slammed his hands on the table and he sounded like he was g-growling?

"Shut your mouth before I put a hole in your face!" He said. Laney suddenly stopped eating and didn't feel as comfortable anymore. But now that i've noticed it, there was something oddly endearing about Seth and Lane. Even though they're siblings, they did look much closer on a deeper level. I wonder what that was? Should I want to know?

"Seth stop it...I'm used to it." Lane whispered dejectedly. 'No its not okay!" Seth cried out. "I'm sick of this little shit always riding our asses!" He cried out making Kyle snap out of it and stand up to. Here I was, trying to enjoy some free lunch on a day off of school. And this was already happening, first Tanaka and now this. I think i'm just going to go now. I slowly got off of my chair, hoping to go by unnoticed especially by Dean and started leaving the table. As I left, I noticed that they were still bickering about something. But all I knew was that I wanted no part of it, no wonder

Americans were looked down on around the world. I took one pause when i'm at the door, noticing that a lot of the Japanese folk were either looking like they were encouraging the fight. Or were upset about, it was then that I noticed that Dean looked my way and stood up, about to make his way towards me.

I spun around and walked off, no longer wanting any part of that mess. I might bump into them at school later but right now I really ha to worry about how I was going to get back home. I still couldn't orientate myself around the city. And I really needed to find my dad's company so that he could take me back. I glanced down at the watch on my wrist and it was already a quarter to one. I frowned, while sighing heavily as I noted that I missed lunch already.

"Need some help?" I jumped at the deep voice behind me, and I turned around almost getting whiplash. I gulped when I noticed how close Dean and I were.

"I-uh, like I said before. I need to find my dad's company. " I said while shurgging my shoulders. "I still don't know where my house is. And i'm a little lost." I half smiled, and half chuckled.

"I can try to help you. Don't you have a phone number that you can call your dad in and everything?" I shook my head at him.

"I don't have service in Japan yet. He's been pretty busy himself with the company and all. I don't even know what he does in his job. We were never really that close to begin with at home, and now we're like strangers." I shrugged at him sheepishly. Dean hummed, "but I did take a picture of the name of his company so i'm hoping that'll suffice?" I asked him while pulling out my phone and showing him the picture of it. Dean nodded, "yeah I can take you, lets go." He said, while taking my arm in his hand and dragging me forward. But when he did touch me, I felt a sharp wave of sparks shot up my arm making me gasp hoarsely and pulling out my arm away from him.

Dean's eyes widened just as much as I did. "Man, that electrical current is so strong here in Japan…" I said while rubbing my arm where I felt the sparks fly. "It must be from all the technology around here. It could be a lose wire or something." It was the first time I saw Dean smile all day. That stoic, and hard expression on his face that he wore suddenly melted in a really nice smile? Wait, what was I saying? I'm not gay snap out of it Lark. I shook my head, but Dean was still smiling brightly. He looked like a completely different person from sternness that i've seen at the shop. Wait, now that I think of it…

"What are you going to do about your friends? Are you going to leave them there to fight in the middle of the restaurant?" I asked him, but Dean wouldn't stop smiling at me and I was getting creeped out by it. First, he was all so serious and now this?

"They'll be fine, they're always like that besides they get it over it eventually. We need to find your dad remember?" I nodded dumbly and then we set off walking down the busy, warm day of Sapparo. But I couldn't help but wonder, why was he suddenly so interested in helping me? We hardly know each other. As we passed through Sapparo, Dean started pointing out the important historical monuments. And he even started pointing out the most popular places to go to Japan. Saying how we should meet up again and show them to me. I couldn't help but agree to that, they all looked so cool. And I was glad that I was able to have the opportunity to see more of Japan than I thought. The ditch day, was turning out better than I originally thought.

I'm sure i'm probably going to get my ass eaten by my dad when he finds out I wasn't able to go and that I missed class. But hey, you can't entirely put that blame on me. After all, I was still new to Japan more than my dad.

And I couldn't find my way around just yet. Japan was huge, bigger than I originally thought and it really wasn't that bad. Sure, I was surrounded by a foreign race in which I had problems communicating to. But I had the opportunity to make new friends, and even learn a language. Something that I could cross off my bucket list.

Dean and I kept looking around Japan until we finally were at the building that I was looking for. My dad's company. I gulped as we stood in front of the large building, I couldn't help but feel nervous about it. Dad has never told me what he did for a living, and he never really wanted to talk about his work in the first place. I didn't know how he was going to react to my showing up at his building with now reason or without a cause to it.

"Well, this is it...I hope you find whatever it is you're looking for Lark." Dean said, while shoving his hands inside his front pockets. He almost looked like he didn't want to leave me in an unknown building. And I couldn't help but have an idea pop into my head. "Hey Dean?" I asked, turning to face him. Dean looked at me with a weird look in his eyes again. "Want to come with?" I asked while grunting my throat, trying to not look like a little pussy. Dean smiled again and nodded in agreement. But as we went inside the building, I couldn't help but notice that there was something. I looked down, and noticed that Tanaka's Daddy contract was missing.

I'm screwed as fuck. Oh well.

Family Matters

The building stood tall and intimidating the more I stared at it.

Around me, the sounds of the busy city life grew dull as nerves started settling in the pit of my stomach. I gulped harshly, trying to block out the sounds of the city streets behind me and the feeling of being engulfed by a crowd of people. The only sound that I could hear was the sound of my own heart beating. "Lark, are you alright?" Dean asked softly, snapping me out of whatever haze I was in. I've never heard him talk like that before. His voice is normally deep and authoritative. Even though I've only known for a few hours, that was the impression that he gave me. He was intimidating to everyone who hears him.

I didn't want to admit it, but I was scared of my father sometimes. We never had a close bond growing up, even after my mom died. Families were normally supposed to feel closer when stuff like that happens. But nope, not with my dad. He just decided to delve into work. I could only guess that it was his way of coping with mom's death. And let work consume him, he hardly has time for me anymore. He barely even knows that I exist. He's the only family that I have, but I still feel invisible. I suddenly felt those same sparks on my arm again making me jump a little out of my trance. I looked down at Dean's warm and calloused hand. And I don't know why but all the insecurities I had before dimmed a bit. All I could feel and see was him, what was wrong with me? Why did I feel like this? I've never felt like this toward another boy before...

He arched a brow at me, as if expecting an answer from me. I gulped, and shook my head to get rid of these thoughts in my head. "Y-yeah, lets go." I muttered, stepping in front of him and towards the swinging doors ahead. People were looking at us oddly probably wondering why two teenagers weren't at school especially two White teenagers. They were all dressed in a professional attire, one that we both lacked in. I looked left and right and all around me, surprised that my dad worked in a company like this.

"You sure your dad works here?" Dean asked gawking at the place himself.

"Yeah, positive." I nodded to him, as I took a couple of daring footsteps up to the front desk. Hoping that the pretty Japanese woman would know some English.

"Hello, how can I help you two today?" She said with a slight accent. I nearly melted in relief. "Hi, I'm looking for my father. He works here, you don't happen to know a man called Mark Myers do you?" The lady raised her eyebrows in surprise.

"Yes, he's the owner of this company! I'm surprised he has a son. He's never mentioned that he has before." She said. Making me freeze, and my body stiffen. Does he really not appreciate me as a son?

"A-anyways could you call him? I need to talk to him." I told her sheepishly. The kind lady nodded and dialed a number in the phone, she hummed every now and then as someone from the other line finished what they seem to say. And then she hung up and cleared her throat.

"Are you sure your his son?" She asked making me frown and cross my brows... "Yeah, very sure." I answered.

"He's never mentioned anything about having family before. Its not even on his file." I suddenly felt cold and stiff as a wave of embarrassment washed over me. It was almost like a chunk of ice went down my spine, and it didn't help that Dean was a few inches behind me, listening in on the conversation. It made me feel smaller than I already am, and I'm only 5'3.

"Anyways, he should be out of a meeting he's having soon. You can wait in the seating area..." She pointed out, making me nod my head in thanks as I walked towards Dean first. "Hey, uhm...you don't have to hang around anymore. My dad's gunna' come any minute now so you're free to go? I guess, thanks?" I said dumbly, making him smile anyway.

"I'd rather stay and make sure you get home safe." Dean said with that same tone in his voice that made my body react unnaturally. I gulped and nodded."Sure, whatever floats your boat I guess." I answered with a shrug, Dean smiled again and sat down next to me.

It was quiet for 15 minutes until we heard a few loud voices coming from around the corner. Dean and I's head whipped toward the sound that was echoing off the walls. My dad was rounding the corner with a lot of people on his side. All dressed in fancy pants business attire.

I gulped suddenly feeling small against them all. I am 5'4 short for a guy in general. And skinny too. Sometimes i wished i had more meat on my bones like Dean's muscles. I would attract the ladies more...wait now I'm going off topic again.

My father stood in the middle of the group who chatted among themselves anxiously. My father was a busy and popular man....

"Mr. Meyers!" My dad and I whipped our head to see the voice of the same nice Japanese lady trying to call his attention.

She clumsily walked up to him with a stack of papers in her hand and in a hushed tone. She then made a pointed gesture to me making me stiffen when my dad glanced my way with a stern look on his face.

Crap.Double crap.

I gulped feeling my hands shake and my heart rate pick up. Dean, who was suddenly beside me brushed his fingers along mine. I didn't want to look at him, I felt embarrassed for being scared of my dad. It almost felt like Dean wanted to hold my hand.

I gulped again when my father started sauntering forward leaving the group behind him. "Why are you not in school and who's this?" He asked angrily.

"I-I-.." why did my throat suddenly close up again? Why couldn't I breathe? "He got lost on his way home. He was late to school and the closed the gates on him. We met on the way here I'm Dean." Dean finished for me while taking out his hand and expecting a handshake. My dad, however, looked displeased and disgusted by it. And ignored the handshake.

My eyes widened at that and Dean was now the one who didn't look too pleased, I could see the muscles in his jaw line locking. Even as he put his hand back down at his side.

"I see." My dad said while gritting his teeth. " And why didn't you call me yourself hours ago?" Did he just growl a little? I gulped.

"I-I don't have your number dad. You never gave it to m-me." My dad looked like he was thinking really hard about something before nodding.

"I see. Must have slipped my mind, i'll talk to the school about your absence today and then we'll talk at home. Wait here for me in the mean time I'm almost done with the meeting."

I felt like I was slapped. Dad never cared about me, he didn't even ask me how my day was, i'll take you home myself and he didn't even give me his number.

"You can go back to where you came from. You're done here." He said to Dean. Why was he treating him like that? And why did I care so much about it? Even though I know this is stupid, we just met but I didn't want him to go.

As my dad turned around and walked away I stopped Dean from leaving to. Everyone around me always left and I was used to it by now, should be used to it. But something told me that this time I wanted someone to stay. The moment I touched Dean I felt the sparks again that made me feel oddly warm.

"Stay?" I asked softly making Dean smile brightly at me as he didn't hesitate to hold my hand this time. Now that my dad was gone. Why wasn't I pushing it away? I am straight aren't I? Why did I like it when he held my hand? What's wrong with me? Dean eyes softened when he looked at me in a way that no one had before. Not my dad, not even my mom when she was alive.

"Always." He whispered as we took our seats in the lobby. For some reason, I couldn't bring myself to care about the Japanese people who were whispering about us, two white boys holding hands. I didn't want to let go of it. It made me feel safe.

I was scared to let it go. It didn't look like he was going to at any minute because he latched onto it even more tightly. Making me smile in relief.I couldn't shake off the feeling though, that someone was watching us from a distance. I didn't want to think so hard about it and just enjoyed holding a boy's hand.

Maybe I'm not so straight as I thought I was. And that scares me.

A/N: Another update tomorrow guys, let me know what you think. :)

Family Matters Part 2

Dean's POV:

The moment Lark didn't let go off my hand, I knew that we were mates. He may not be a werewolf, but I knew that even as a human he felt the bond. The connection.

He may be human, but even humans feel the connection. Despite not knowing what the connection fully meant. They feel it. My hard exterior softened as my soul mate, the one I've been waiting for..for years is now with me. And it looks like he has problems with his dad, an alpha werewolf of a small pack in America. Why was he here in Japan? The alpha sensed that I too was a werewolf, and he wasn't too happy with the fact that his son is my mate. But why was he human? Shouldn't he be a werewolf as well? Is his father hiding something from him?

My pack and I are here because we suspect rogue vampires are on the loose in Japan. Killing humans to fill their blood lust. And as second in command, my alpha sent me and my closest companions to handle the job while he stays in America. Lark's father and I are going to have to have a long chat though. I intend to take Lark back with me to America.

Lark suddenly stiffened beside me, and as promised I didn't leave his side. I held his hand firmer in my own, and dared to trace small circles inside his palm with my thumb. He relaxed with my touch making me smile. But then, a dreadful scent struck my nose a rogue vampire was nearby.

My brow arched when Lark felt the presence of him nearby too...but how? Is Lark a human or a werewolf? Who was his mother?"You okay?" I asked him softly. I'm normally known for my rough exterior and my serious nature. But when it comes to my mate all that changed.

"Yeah...I just can't shake the feeling of someone watching me.." I gulped, he was right. I took a sharp intake of the air and picked up the scent.

It was Tanaka Raizo. A rogue vampire. My inner wolf was growling, and I couldn't help but agree with him. What was Raizo doing here? Unless. ..no. It can't be, he couldn't want my mate's blood. The mere thought of that made my own blood boil. Before coming to Japan, my alpha sent me and my friends to chase down a group of rogue vampires that are killing humans and drinking their blood. The news reported that there was a mass murderer on the loose, but my alpha and I knew better. As beta, I was told to memorize certain scents by my alpha and be on the guard for him. Raizo was on the list. I didn't think, however, that on my mission I would find my mate. That complicates things even more. But even then, I would have to talk to my father on taking him back with me to America where he belongs.

That also meant, that I would have to talk to his father...who was a were-wolf. But what I don't understand is, why isn't my mate one? Why is he a human? Who was his mother really?

"Dean?" My head snapped away from my train of thought, it went from the direction of where Tanaka's scent was in and down to my mate. I smiled at him. Suddenly feeling all my worries slip away just by looking at him."Yeah?" I asked.

"Is something wrong? You've been quiet." Lark questioned. "I'm alright, just thinking about you is all." And I really was, I let out a small laugh when I saw a blush rise up on his cheeks and he looked down quickly. And he thought that he was straight, I shook my head. He tried taking out his hand in mine but I latched onto it refusing to let it go. Even when his father came back around without his business partners. His eyes narrowed at me at first and then they went down to our hands.

"Lark my assistant will lead you to my office. I'll take you home in a bit, and we'll be having our conversation later." His dad said sternly, making my wolves' hackles rise up defensively. Without really noticing it, his father was threatening my mate. I didn't want to let him go and leave him alone. But what can I? He doesn't know about werewolves or mates, he's just a human.

"Bye." Lark whispered softly, and this time I regrettably let go of his hand. His father and I waited a few more minutes until we knew that his assistant guided him out of the lobby until he stepped forward.

"What is another werewolf doing in Japan? I thought this are was clear of any more of them! I don't want my son involved!" He whispered harshly under his breath.

"Why not? I believe you already know that he and I are mates. Why isn't he one of us? Who is mother?" I hissed at him.

"That is no business of yours." He growled. "Look, Mike is it? Do you smell what I smell?" I asked him harshly. Making him scrunch up his eyebrows in confussion. "There's a vampire here isn't there?" He whispered lowly.

"Tanaka Raizo, that fucker." Mike cursed loudly. "I bet you he is listening to this conversation within' an ear shot from us right now." I nodded.

"That's right. What does he want with my mate?" I growled.

"I don't know, that's why I've been trying to keep him away from Lark for so long. All I know is that he is a cop here in Japan, but a rogue vampire that doesn't pertain to any affiliated clan. He's dangerous, and I think he has a blood lust for my son." He said with an exasperated sigh.

"Where is your pack?" I asked him. "Can't you keep Lark safe with them? You know vampires wouldn't dare to break the treaty by crossing borders." I said loud enough to make sure Raizo heard. "No, mine is in America...I only have a few pack members here in Japan with me on business with the rogue situation. I kept him away from my pack because I don't want Lark to be involved in our world yet."

"He's not a werewolf is he?" I asked him disappointedly. "He is...but he hasn't shifted yet, that's his wolf can't sent yours yet. But your wolf can sense it in him." I nodded, understanding his situation.

"What are you going to do until then?" I asked him. "Not only do we have an issue with Raizo, but Lark's heat is coming up soon." I warned him urgently.

"What if he stays with me and my friends for awhile, he'll be safe with me." I urged him while stepping forward. "I'll keep him safe." His father hesitated for a moment but he nodded.

"Fine, he'll be safer with you than with me. I'm already doing such a bad job in raising him anyways." He said glumly.

"I don't think he'll mind it." His father said. "I hope not. He claims that he is straight though..." I said with a smirk making him laugh and nod his head in disagreement. "I know that my son is not straight. But for some reason, I am okay with it. He just needs to learn to accept himself. After all, he's the only family I have left. I just don't know how else to keep him safe now that this Raizo is after his tail." He said, making me frown.

"What are you going to tell him though? About him coming to live with me from now on, a total stranger." I huffed, he only shrugged. "I'll make something up, just leave that to me. I only ask that you give me a day with him, then you can take him." He said, and I couldn't help but agree to that reasonable request.

"I'll give you my number then." I told him and he nodded as he too slipped out his cell as we exchanged numbers.

"I want my son safe. I know I look harsh with him, but I have my reasons." He said making me nod understandingly. "Yeah, I know..." I said, "Tell Lark I'll see him soon." I told him as I turned around ready to leave.

"Wait, one more thing." I cocked my head over my shoulder. "Yes?" I asked.

"Thank you for dropping off my son..." He said, "and I apologize if my behavior earlier was rash. I don't want to come off on bad terms with my future son in law." He said with a smile, making me smile back.

"No worries, no offenses were taken." I said as we shook hands respectively. I waited till he arched a brow and turned around and back to Lark. I know we'll see each other again soon, I can feel it. However, once I stepped outside of the building the scent of the vampire disappeared. I frowned, took out my phone and hit the speed dial...

"Are you aware of the time zone changes you neandrathal?" My alpha barked snarkily, making me roll my eyes. He wasn't a morning person.

"There's a problem...we found the rogue vampire." I told him...the sounds on the other end of the phone were like cackling noises and staticky as I heard him shuffle out of the bed. His business voice going back on. He sounded more alert this time. "Good, we're at the right place then..you know what to do right?" The alpha said with a morning rasp in his voice.

"Yes, but there's another issue this vampire is after my mate's blood." I told him. I heard cussing on the other side. "Fuck, congrats on finding your mate man finally. Now I need to find my own mate, but be careful. Don't let your instincts take over when he's around or whenever you see him. They're dangerous, and unpredictable." He said seriously, making me scoff.

"I'm not scared of no vampire, they should be scared of us." I told him making him laugh. "For your mate's safe you should be." He warned.

"Yeah, I know..." I whispered.

"We have to find those rogue vampires and finish them. And remember about what I said with your mate's heat?"

"Yeah, yeah..."

"Don't lose control of your wolf. Right now its getting antsy now that its found its mate, and that its in danger." The alpha said.

"I'm hanging up." He said and true to his word he did.

Lark's POV:

My feet tapped anxiously against the floor as I sat and waited in his office for a long time now. What was he talking about with Dean? I gulped and took a drink of water from the cup that the nice secretary brought for me. The door suddenly opened and slammed shut making me jump and nearly spill my water all over my pants.

Great.

"Sorry..." Dad said as he pointedly noticed the almost accident. Wait, did he just say sorry? He never does... "So...Dean?" I asked, unsure why all that I could think of now was Dean. "Look son, we need to talk." Oh no, the last time we had one of those talks was when mom died. And that didn't go so well, it ended up with my crying like a girl.

"What's up dad?" I asked nervously. "I know you and I never really got a chance to talk since mom passed away, and I guess I can only blame myself for it. I raised my eyebrows, what brought this on all of a sudden? He never gets into the deep stuff with me. He never has the time for that anymore.

"But, son, its also my fault that I didn't tell you about the academy's rules thoroughly or given you your American passport. Or my phone number ...but there are things that you don't understand in life yet."

"What? I'm so confused, what are you saying exactly? What's going on?" I felt panic begin to swell in m. And I found myself wishing that Dean is still here.

"What I'm trying to say is, that its okay to like boys son." No! I don't like boys! I'm not gay i'm straight.

"No! You're wrong!" I said angrily while getting up from my chair, and letting it fall behind me. "I don't like guys, I'm normal I'm straight!" I argued. My dad started laughing a little, "anybody who has to reassure themselves that they are straight are not really straight son." He said, I can feel the weight crashing down on my shoulders, as my eyes started brimming red around the edges.

I was trying really hard not to cry. As my chest swelled with a pang of embarrassment.

"You don't know me well enough to say that! We never talk anymore!" I spat at him, making his eyes cast down on his desk.

"I know son, but I see the way that boy looks at you and the way you've held hands." He said pointedly.

"That means nothing!" I cried out desperately, as my chest started dry heaving. "You, y-you what do you know!?" I said hysterically, trying not to breakdown. "Your never around anymore, you don't know how hard these past few days have been for me dad. Trying to live in a new country, where nothing is in English! I hardly have any friends here and its just so hard!" I said with a choked up sob while kicking his desk. Everything felt like it was falling apart. I couldn't handle this anymore. I let out a sob, suddenly feeling pathetic and miniscule. Dad shot his head up in alarm as he got up from his desk and did the one thing he hasn't done in a long time.

He hugged me.

He held my face to my chest as I let out ugly dry heaving sobs.

"You only think about yourself! You never once asked me if I wanted to come to Japan or not. You just dragged me here." I whimpered. "I miss my friends, my old school...I miss the life I had back there." I said while I hiccuped again.

I slammed my fists into his chest but he only held onto me even more tightly. "I know, I know its my fault. I'm sorry son..." He said with a sigh as I continued to ugly cry. Somebody walked into the room but I couldn't bare to look and see who it was. The lady gasped behind me "sorry for interrupting." She was about to close the door when dad stopped her.

See what I mean? He never gives a damn about me, I wish my mom was still alive. I tried pushing myself away from him but he latched on to me.

"Sarah, cancel my schedule for the rest of today and tomorrow. I'm going to spend some time with my son." He said firmly.

"But sir, the 2 o'clock meeting?" She pressed.

"Cancel it, cancel everything. My son and I are going home." Sarah excused herself out and when I heard the door click shut my dad put his finger under my chin and lifted my head to meet his.

"I didn't know how rough it was for you since mom died I'm sorry. I believe me or not, but since your mother died the only way I can cope with it is through work. It kept my mind off of it." He said, making me scoff.

"It kept your mind off of me too, I bet." Making him wince.

"That too sadly. Son, I really do mean it though...it's okay to like boys." He said reassuringly. "You just need to learn to accept and embrace that part of yourself." I scoffed, why is it that no one thinks I'm straight?

"Can we go home now, I'm tired..." I told him, making him nod as he grabbed his leather messenger bag and car keys, he looked door on our way out of his office as we walked past the friendly secretary who waved goodbye and frowned when she saw how red my face was from crying.

We passed the swinging doors and was about to go into his car when I stopped him, remembering Dean.

"Where's Dean?" I asked worriedly, making him smirk and shake his head at me. "You'll see each other again soon." He reassured while ruffling my hair, something he hasn't done for me since I was a kid.

"Stop...." I said as we slid into the car, with him on the driver's side.

"And you say you don't like boys and you're already worried about Dean?" He asked while starting the engine of the car. I scoffed and rolled my eyes.

Dean is just a cool dude, the only guy that I care for...somewhat.

A/N: Poor Lark :(

In the Dark

- -

A/N: Poll : Tanaka or Dean? :)

It was pretty dark outside when my dad and I scrolled up around the neighborhood, and we were also quiet.

"Dad?" He hummed as he gave me a sideways glance. "Never mind." I answered back, I didn't want to wear him out more than I already did. My dad sighed as we pulled into the garage space and put the veichle in park. He smiled ruefully at me when he clicked open his seat belt and got out of the car. I sighed at the awkwardness again, and got out of the car slowly, carefully.

"I've never told you this son...but I do miss your mother you know." He whispered as he got the keys out of his front pocket and opened the door with a screech, making me cringe. "Never thought you didn't, you just had a different way of coping with things, and worked." He chuckled.

"When did you get so smart?" He teased, making me roll my eyes. "Wasn't I always smart?" He laughed at that strolled inside the house, kicking the door shut and closed it with his keys. "So, about Dean..." He drawled, making me groan I really didn't want to have this talk with him.

"Dad...." I drawled. "Can we not? Let's just go to bed and talk later yeah? I'm beat." My dad chuckled and ruffled my hair playfully, making me swat his hand away in annoyance. "Don't, I'm not five." I whined.

"You'll always be five to me son." He chuckled while pinching my cheeks and heading up the stairs to bed. I sighed at that, and went back to my room, I didn't bother switching the light on and closed the door shut. I let out a big yawn and stretch as I took of my first article of clothing, my shirt. Wow, I'm so boring.

"Beautiful." I nearly jumped out of my skin at the voice in the corner.

"Who's there!?" I cried out as my hands started to involuntarily shake. The dark figure in the corner of the room stepped into the ghost of the moonlight and I didn't know whether or not to be relieved or scared even more than I already was. It was Tanaka Raizo, I gulped.

"W-what are you doing here?" I asked. "You d-do k-know this is private property r-right? Its against the law." I was pretty sure that it was against the law in any country to sneak into anybody's home in general. It had to be common knowledge right?

"Your window, was an open invitation for me Lark-kun." He said as he stepped forward, making me take a few steps back from him.

I was scared, I felt threatened int he confinements of my own bedroom. A place where you were supposed to feel safe. In the bravest voice I could muster I told him, "you n-need to l-leave." I told him, cursing myself for how shaky my voice sounded.

"Are you sure that's what you want?" He asked, stepping forward, with a stride in his step. "What was with this guy? I always knew there was something wrong with him since the day I meet him."

"You never did give me an answer to my proposition over the contract, boy." I gulped, "Its been two day. I n-need time." To be honest, I was just trying to figure out a way to say no to him without getting killed.

"I need an answer now." He whispered hotly, with his face really close to mine, unnaturally close. I really wanted him away from me. I had my back against the wall and his arms were on either side of my face. So I did what he wanted, I took a deep breathe and closed my eyes.

"No." I said, listening as he took a sharp inhale of breath. "No? You don't want to be my baby?" He asked as his finger suddenly drew a line from my ear tangent to my jaw. I gulped. "No. I'm not gay, I told you before!"

I was then that he did the most shocking thing ever, he knocked my legs apart and put his knee cap in between them, making me gasp hoarsely. What was he doing? Get off me! He leaned down against my ear lobe and slowly licked my ear? "Are you sure about that? I can make you cum harder than any...woman can." He purred, his leg pushing against me, almost rocking into me. "Get off me. I don't want you here!" I cried out when his leg brushed against something sensitive. That was just a normal body reaction right? I can't possibly be gay. That was the only reason why it could be so sensitive right now.

"Really?" He whispered against my neck as he smelled my neck line? Why was he doing that? I suddenly couldn't stop shaking, I can't fight him off of me, I thought weakly as his hand trailed down my chest further and further until it paused on the waistline of my pants. "Why are you so hard then?" He asked against my earlobe. My eyes widened in shock, no....I...."Its just a r-reaction. I-it doesn't mean anything." I suddenly wished my dad would wake up.

Then, his hand was on it. Right on my bulge, and the strangest most embarrassing sound came out of me. I've never been touched there really.

Sure I've masturbated before but...never this. I didn't want his hand on me.

"Get off me, please..." I whined as my body seemed to think differently. He had this weird ghost of a smile on him as he gave my buldge a little squeeze making me moan, why was this happening to me right now? Why did it feel good? I wasn't gay.

He squeezed the buldge again and hummed. "You're not only hard for me, Lark-kun but you're also wet." He purred as he kissed my neckline. "Don't..t-touch..."my voice seemed to trail off when his hand was suddenly replaced with his kneecap. I let out a hoarse gap at the sensation. His knee cap grinded against my crotch in agonizing circles, making me let out a few whimpers every now and then. "You don't think you're gay, but you're beautiful muscle wants me Lark-kun, and I think you do too." No! I wanted to shout out, I can't fight you off me, you're too strong you're forcing this on me. Anybody else would have a reaction if their being touched like this.

But for some reason, i felt too paralyzed too move, my mind my screaming something else. But my body wanted....needed a release. I couldn't do this, I whimpered, I had to push him off of me. Get my dad's attention somehow.

Then, he did something else....something I really didn't....he unbottened my zipper and no matter how hard i tried to I couldn't move. It was like some unknown force kept me there against the wall. And...my body felt so hot, why?

I let out a moan, as all of a sudden all rationale wiped out of my head when he took his hand in me and kissed my tip. My vision felt hazy when he drew his tounge out and swirled the tip of it back and forth almost as if he were carerrising it. I felt so hot...my body suddenly arched from the wall and into his hand.

"P-please." I whimpered/moaned as he dragged his tongue up and down the trunk of my cock, that was now hard. I get it now, I secretly cried. I wasn't straight anymore, no normal straight guy would enjoy this.

"You still don't want me to be your daddy?" He asked with his dark eyes on me, making me gasp when he blew my tip, and I watched in shock as it twitched to its master. Why was I enjoying this? I should push him away from him.

"Answer me baby boy..." I whimpered when he continued to swirl his hot tongue on my tip. "I-I...I have a dad though.

He chuckled darkly...."the contract boy. " I couldn't think, I couldn't feel anything but the pleasure that his mouth gave on me. "I..."

I gasped and I was a goner. His mouth was completely encompassed around my dick, and he was bobbing his head up and down making me hiss as I tried to shove him off agains but he didn't let me. He grabbed my ass all of a sudden pulling me forward. And he had me all the way in his mouth?? I gasped and let out a wet moan, completely weak to him. I know I should have fought him off...but I felt so good. I wanted...more.

"Call me daddy baby...do it." He demanded making me moan and pant as his teeth suddenly grew sharper? He scraped against my cock, as my heart started pounded loudly against my ribcage I felt so good.

"Daddy!" I cried out as a white hot blaze flushed through me and into his mouth as I came. I moaned loudly as I came again, but he wouldn't let go off my dick, and that...was so hot. He scraped his teeth against my tip again and I came so hard that my stomach started cramping. My legs trembled and I felt like collapsing when he finally let me go and kissed my tip when it went lip. I gulped and panted hoarsely as my back writhed a little against the wall.

He crawled back up to me and kissed me harshly against my lips, letting me taste myself in my kiss as he parted. I licked my lips and stood there shocked with my pants hanging around my ankles. "Remember this every time you're with Dean." He said hoarsely, "remember who made you come so hard you still want more." He purred while twisting a sensitive nipple in between his fingers making me moan. What is going on with my body, what is wrong with me? I panted.

"I can make you sing baby..." He whispered against my ear lobe, and when he flicked his tongue against my ear I let out another moan. My body turning into putty into his hands. Then all of a sudden, the lights turned on and like my brain turned on from the haze of lust, shame filled me when dad stepped into the room.

"Get away from my son!" He growled.

This was so humiliating.

In the Dark part 2

A /N: Two updates in one day!? *gasp* That never happens, happy reading! :D

"Dad...I can explain" I stuttered, my body was still shaking from arousal and it was really awkward, even as I tried to lift up my pants and cover myself as my dad glared at Tanaka Raizo. He held his hand out to me, making me shut my mouth.

"I'm not going to ask again...out of my house, now." He said through gritted teeth. Tanaka clicked his teeth together and held his hands up in a mocking surrender. Tanaka let out a low and hoarse chuckle as he glanced at my dad.

"I want you away from my house, and away from my son Raizo." Tanaka didn't say anything but chuckle throughout the entire time.

"The boy is mine, Meyers. One day he'll be mine, mark my words....and there's no way you can protect him this time." He said while turning around and jumping out of my window. My body was shaking at what he said, what the hell was going on? How did my dad know him?

"Dad!?" I asked, whipping my body around now that I have my pants back on, my arousal long forgotten.

"Dean is on his way. I thought that I could keep you safe here, keep your mother's promise. I was wrong." He said with a sigh as he ran a hand through his hair.

"Dad? You have to tell me, I can't keep up with all these secrets anymore. What's going on? How do you know Tanaka?" I pressed, stalking forward.

"I'll tell you when..." My eyes widened in surprise when I heard a horn toot outside. "He's here already, that's fast." He mumbled something about wolves? "Get your shit together, come with me down stairs."

"Dad, its in the middle of the night though. Where will I go?" He let out a slow sigh and looked at me sadly. "You're going to move in with Dean, you'll be safer there va...his kind can't cross Dean's territory. You'll be safer there than with me." He confessed, making me arch my brow, I have never been more confused in my life.

"Dad!?" I squeaked.

"Don't make me tell you twice, pack your shit. Get ready." I gulped and didn't wait to be told again, I took out my suit case from my closet and started pouring in handfuls of clothing. I heard the door slam shut and a couple of angry voice down stairs. As I was packing, I couldn't help but stop for a bit and peer open my bedroom door to hear who it was. It was Dean. A wave of embarrassment washed over me, as he started yelling at my dad. He was normally really calm around me, I've never seen him like this before.

"You let that blood sucker into this house? What kind of hunter are you!?" He screamed in his face.

Hunter?

"I can smell him all over the place, its disgusting." Dean growled out as a couple of more familiar voices popped into the room.

"Dude, what smells so bad in here?" It was Kyle from the ramen shop! And his sister, and Sean.

"It's you, you idiot." Sean playfully said while slapping him in his shoulder.

"Fuck off fucker!" Kyle spat.

"Kyle don't be a prick." Lane said while batting her long eyelashes at him making him roll his eyes.

"Where is he?" Dean asked my dad all of a sudden. "He's upstairs, getting ready." He mumbled. Dean whipped his head around upstairs and saw me making me go all skittish at the notion of being caught. I froze for a moment, and nearly peed my pants when he glared at me. It was like...like he knows. I gulped and instantly shut the door to my room, and continued packing.I didn't know where the hell I was going to go but I trusted him, I think. How is my dad sending me off to a person that I barely knew for a few days? The door swung open with a bang, making me jump out of my skin I didn't want to turn around and look to know who it was. I gulped as my hands started to shakily put in everything I need.

"He was here." Dean murmured angrily, making me shiver. "Uhhh...y-ye ah." I whispered nervously.

"I can smell him." He growled, smell him? Okay? Did he smell bad or something?

He took two large strides forward until his he was right behind me. "I can smell him all over you, and I don't like it." He growled again making me gulp. He flipped me around, and I gasped in shock by the suddenness of it.

"I don't like that he touched you. Did you like it? Did you like having his filthy hands on you?" Dean said, his voice sounded murderous. Was it wrong that I did?

"I...I..."

"That will change." He whispered lowly, looking down to my lips, making me gulp. Was I going to get raped again? Twice in one night? That wasn't fair.

"For now, we need to talk things through with your dad." He murmured angrily, while closing my suit case shut for me and bringing it down stairs and having no choice or say in the matter, I followed him.

"Ayyyyee, how's it goin' Lark!" Sean said while slapping my shoulder on the back. "Fuck man, you reek of that fucking blood suc-" He caught himself off. "I mean, you just really stink dude." He said. I rolled my eyes, maybe I do need a shower. I sniffed my arm a bit but didn't smell what they smelled for some reason.

"So dad, mind clueing me in here?" I asked forcibly. Dad let out a sigh, "fine you were going to find out when you were 18, it was your mother's wish but now is as good as a time anyways." He said while nodding his head towards the basement, Dean still looked mad at me he wasn't talking to me at all.

As the door opened I was stunned at what I saw, everywhere I looked different types of weapons were stored on the wall. What did my dad do for a living again? I gulped...."You've always wondered about my day job, so here it is. I run a business for the elite VHA." He said sternly as everyone else looked at me.

"And that is??" I asked him. "Vampire hunter association." He repeated. My eyes widened, as I gulped...."V-vampires?"

He nodded.

"But...." I whispered.

"Let me finish, I'm a human and I own a business here in Japan to train elite vampire hunters in the area. I also own one in America, but the main reason why we moved here is because there has been a bunch of rogue vamp sightings here in the country. We think the cause of all the mysterious death link back to Tanaka Raizo's clan." He said, making my blood run cold. I couldn't catch a break here could I? All this happened just for missing one day at school? Fuck.

"If he's a vampire...then..."

"I'm a werewolf, and so are they." Dean finished for me while pointing at his friends who waved happily at me.

"Don't worry, we're here to protect you." Kyle said while puffing out his chest.

"I know this is a lot of information to handle son, too much to take in just one day, night really. But, Tanaka is getting to close to you, we don't know what his motives are but..."

"Obviously he wants his penis." Sean said darkly, making me blush. Dean frowned at my reaction.

"What other reason is there? He's a horn dog."

"Shut the fuck up Sean, you're an idiot." Lane snapped. "Yeah, but I'm not the one fucking my brother am I?" Sean fired back. Lane recoiled as though she's been slapped.

"Take that back..." Kyle growled out. "I'm sick of you always ragging on us all the time." Sean rolled his eyes.

"At least I have a mate!" Kyle snapped back making Dean scowl at their childish antics. "Enough!" Dean snapped at them.

"You want to start something? Take it outside, now is not the time!" He growled at them who nodded submissively. Wow, that was effective. I thought to myself, though I couldn't help but feel bad for Lane. I bet she gets a lot of shit for wait...mate?

"What's a...m-mate?" I asked as they all whipped their heads towards me. "We'll talk about that when you get to my place yeah?" He said while strolling forward and cupping my face in his hands. I nodded softly feeling dumb struck by how soft his eyes were compared to how hard they've been moments ago.

"Y-yeah. Dad?" I asked craning to look at him as Dean dropped his hands, making the warm tingle I felt earlier go away.

"Yes, anyways back to my original point. Before I was interrupted." He said looking pointedly at the other four.

"We have a plan about these rogue vampires, but its risky. You're the inheritance to my companies Lark." I blinked dumbly, me? I-I'm only sixteen! I can barely do calculus how am I going to run a company?

I licked my lips dryly. "And?" I asked. "Since Tanaka seems so taken with you, we have a trap that can lure him in. You."

"Me? How? What can I do?" I asked suddenly not liking where this is going.

"I don't like this plan, but you're going to seduce him." Dean said angrily with his fists clentched. "What!?" I screeched. "Noooo...I can't do that!"

"I can't seduce anybody!"

"You're going to seduce him, and kill him son." My dad said while looking at me firmly, as if I had no other choice.

Why me? I didn't even want to kill Tanaka in the first place...he helped me out so much in Japan and....and, I licked my lips was it bad that I liked him? Was it bad that I liked his touch? The way he made me call him daddy, the way he grabbed me.

I shook my head and ignored those intrusive thoughts at the task at hand. "Why can't you do it yourself? You seem more experienced at this than me." I asked my dad while frowning.

"You see...that's the problem. He'll suspect me, but he won't suspect you. He's quite fond of you." Dad said with a frown, as he took something out of a drawer.

"Take this with you." My eyes widened when I looked at the dagger. "W-what is that for?"

Why am I so stupid?

"To kill him, black glass is the only way to kill a vampire. Strike him in the heart when you get the chance to, and he'll be gone." My dad said as I carefully took the dagger in my hand. I gulped and put it in my pocket as if it were a phone.

"Okay, I'll do it." I had to kill Tanaka, I had no choice to.

Dean was looking at me carefully as if trying to read me.

"We'll talk more about the plans in the future." Dad said as he pressed a button on the wall that made the weapons disappear behind the wall.

"Okay..." I whispered sadly, not liking the idea of having to kill someone.

"Come on Lark, we got to go." Dean said while taking my arm in his as he escorted me out of the basement and out of my house. Dad stood in the front of the house as he waved goodbye as we rode off in Dean's green jeep wrangler.

There were two other cars following behind us, and I could only assume that it were the other three werewolves behind us.

"You...don't seem surprised that I'm a werewolf." Dean murmured as he placed a hand on my knee, making the familiar spark of tingles shot up my leg. My mind instantly flashed back to how Tanaka used to do the same thing. But I pushed his hand away, and I didn't do that this time. Maybe I am gay.

I gulped. "Yeah...well that's because of fanfiction you know, and anime. They write about stuff like that a lot." I whispered, feeling embarrassed all of a sudden. Dean laughed at that "I thought you would be scared of this. I'm still not happy about Tanaka you know?"

I gulped, "yeah...wouldn't blame you."

"I'm going to have to fix that scent on you. You reek of him, and I don't like that." Dean glowered as he pulled around a corner.

"Fix that?" I asked.

Dean smiled at me as he pulled up another curb, and then it suddenly dawned on me on what he was implying. My face has never turned more red than it did just now.

Please Read~~

HAPPY NEW YEAR!!!

Sorry to disappoint you all, this is not really an update.

I just wanted to say I hope you all have a very happy New Year!

It has been another amazing year on wattpad. If you're alone right now, know that you have a wattpad family with you :D. 2018, may not have been a great year for most of us, it hasn't been that great even for me. If that's the case, be thankful that you had another year of life, there has been many bumps in the roads. But hopefully 2019 will be a better year! 2019 to the wattpad world, would mean more updates on my stories and maybe even a new one would come out. I just wanted to wish you guys a good one, and I hope you're all safe and sound with your friends or family or even on wattpad!

I promise to do more updates next year~~love pointlessxwriter.

Run with the Wolves

<hr>

I 've been running through the jungle, I've been running with the wolves, to get to you. To get to youuuu~~~~~

Dean's 2006 jeep wrangler drove at full seep as we speed past the trees with a couple of cars a few feet behind us. Kyle, and Lane were in one car while Sean was in the other. Dean was quiet as he kept one hand locked on the steering wheel, it was 1 am in the morning, where are we going?

I let out a gasp when a sudden thud was heard on the back of the car, making me whip me head around, "relax it's just Kyle." Dean muttered, I relaxed slightly and looked at him."Where are we going?" I slowly asked him while playing with the hem of my shirt.

"My place, right now its the safest for you here. " He mumbled as he spun the car around so that it passed another tree, it looked like he wasn't going to slow down anytime soon enough. Just a moment ago, I was living a normal life in San Fransisco. I pulled off average grades in school, barely making it with C's. I had my friends and now in Japan I've stumbled upon the discovery of vampires and werewolfs, and my father being a vampire hunter himself. Gritting my teeth, I sucked my bottom lip in my mouth.

Feeling frustrated with the turn of the events that had happened in only a few days.

"Vampires do not cross our borders...we have patrols surrounding the area. Tanaka won't get anywhere near you, I can promise you that." Dean assured me while grasping the steering wheel tightly just by the mention of his name. "Tanaka would have to be stupid enough too even dare set foot onto our ground." I nodded, not finding the will in me to say anything because I was afraid that if I say anything at all it will anger him. So I thought of a diversion instead.

"You said, that they don't cross your borders...what do you mean?" I asked curiously.

"Its simple, its part of the treaty that us werewolves have had with the vampires years ago. We don't cross their territory, they don't cross ours. I'll tell you the history of it when you're ready." I nodded, gazing at the pathway in front of us as the car started slowing down, signaling that we were nearing his pack house. It was simple to look at, a log cabin surrounded by tall trees and bushes I would have never spotted it before if they haven't lead me to where they live. "Normally whenever we bring a human guest here, we'd have to blind fold them." Dean said seriously, making my heart skip a beat at the idea of being blindfolded. "I'm just joking, we don't have any human friends come here. You're the only exception." He said seriously as he opened the garage door and parallel parked perfectly as Kyle and Lucy's car parked evenly on either side. Dean put the car in park, took out his seat belt and stepped out of the car. Not before leaning down and telling me "its safe to come out now you know. You're with the werewolves. We won't bite." He said smiling, as I shakily nodded at his sarcasticness.

"Finally, home!" Lucy exclaimed excitedly while clapping her hands. "That means food." Kyle popped out of the car soon after and stared at her with the most softest expression I have ever seen him wear. He must have really loved her. However, his soft expression dissapeared when Sean showed up "you're such a fat ass always thinking about food. Why can't you be a normal girl and have a salad instead?" I could tell that by the look on Kyle's face he was going to snap at Sean, but it looked like Lucy clearly could hold her own as Sean poked her on one of her ams. "Bite me Sean! Don't be such a dick!" She exclaimed, as Kyle laughed. The trio walked into the house, still being loud as Dean shook there head at them and grabbed my bags out of the trunk. "Are they always like that?" I asked, Dean nodded.

"What's the deal with Sean and Lucy?" I asked, feeling honestly curious about them.

"Well, honestly, before finding out that Lucy was Kyle's mate Sean really liked Lucy. At first, there was a lot of tension between the three of them because as you've already figured out Lucy and Kyle are siblings." I froze in misstep, siblings? "Don't look at me like that Lark...in the werewolf community, the goddess doesn't place any limits on soul mates. Love is love." He said while smiling at me, making me blush like a girl. "So, do you still think you're straight yet?" He whispered, making my body go rigid. To be honest, after what Tanaka Raizo did the other night I was convinced that I wasn't so straight anymore. "No..." I whispered, while staring at him and Dean responded by grinning madly. "Good." He growled lowly, making something in belly start swimming in excitement. The moment we stepped into the house, Dean set his bags down on the carpet as we approached the living room. The others were in the kitchen area, Lucy headed straight for the chocolate. I smiled, watching them interact like children.

"How are you all real?" I whispered to myself, and as if they all heard me their heads whipped to me. Lucy stopped eating.

"What do you mean?" She said with a mouthful of chocolate, "Lucy, love, how many times do I have to tell you not to eat with your mouth full.

Chocolate is not real food." Kyle scolded as he grabbed a napkin and started wiping the sides of her mouth. "Stop hovering mom." She said while batting her hands at her mate.

"We're real." I sighed, as I stood awkwardly in front of them. "That's not what I meant, how are werewolves or vampires even remotely real??" I said while, beginning to pace the room. "I've always had a clear idea of what they are but only through stuff like anime, or manga and crap like that. But if you've guys been real all along why didn't you just come out!? Why are you in hiding??" I yelled at them, feeling the heavy weight of weariness sink down on me. I was tired, and stressed from all of the news.

"Can you imagine if that were to fucking happen?" Sean cursed while hopping down from the kitchen counter and sauntering towards me. "It'll be like the end of the world for you humans an apocalyptic event. We've thought of exposing ourselves to you guys all the time. But if we did that, things will turn ugly real fast. There won't be a solid government anymore, vampires and werewolves will fight for dominance now that the humans 'know' that they're powerless to stop them. Imagine all of the possibilities. To sum it up, we're hiding because unlike you selfish humans we ain't selfish." Sean said, running his fingers through his block locks. I winced, as Dean glared at Sean telling him to shut up with one look.

"I get it." I told Sean as Kyle and Lucy started making their way towards their bed room. "Good night, Lark will see you in the morning." Lucy said while yawning and leaning her body frame on her mate's side as he nodded towards me and Dean while making his way towards one of the bedrooms in the simple log cabin.

"Yeah, I'ma call it a night too. Later, both of you's." Sean said as he took one last look at me with an arched brow as he headed towards a room of his own. Then, it was just me and him my mate. "Sorry if the place isn't as luxurious as your own house." Dean said while getting closer to me so that he was right in front of me, making me gulp at his proximity. "Its fine really." I said as I looked around, trying to avoid his gaze as I gazed at the simple log cabin in the middle of the woods. It was a one story log cabin, with 3 bedrooms, a small kitchen. A warm fireplace and no T.V.

"There's no T.V ?" I asked with an arched brow. "It easier for us to be on the down low, the humans can track us via satellite, we don't have a phone here either so sorry. And if you've noticed your cell doesn't have service here either. Its one of the main reasons why my alpha decided to build this place here."

"So you won't be found. I get it, but how do you make it to school on time then?" I asked, trying to lighten up the mood which appeared to work as he started to bark a laugh. "Simple, we turn and let the wolves run. By car, it'll take three to four hours to get to school." Well, damn. I need to run with the wolves more often then.

Maybe then, I'll never be late to school.

Dangerous Encounters

A/N: This chapter might be confusing, but just a heads up there is a naughty scene up ahead.

Tanaka:

Thirst.

A pain that at first starts low in your belly and slowly crawls up your throat. Until the thirst starts to burn....I wasn't hungry, but a man starved. Starved for something that he can not have but desperately needs for survival. My race and my kind depended on a human's blood to survive. At first sight, Lark's blood called out to me in a way no one else's had before. Any other's blood wouldn't taste the same, and I'd be sick with theirs now I drink only because the clan is watching. Making sure that I don't starve and become a rogue, killing innocents on the streets.

Lately, they've become more dangerous and reckless. And if that problem isn't taken care of, the council will hear about it. I stood in my parked car in the city, doing my duties as an officer fearing that I would never be able to see my Lark-kun again. Not after he was taken by the werewolves. There was no way I would ever be able to see him now that he's being carefully watched. I closed my eyes, my memories floating back to that moment where I held Lark in my hands. I tasted him, smelt him, and his cries were indeed that of a lark bird that night. I groaned internally, remembering him call me daddy.

My hand shakily reached towards my pant line, I haven t done this in so long, I haven't felt the need to since I first tasted it. If his father wouldn't have come in, I would have done more to him. I unbuckled my belt quickly, feeling myself harden uncomfortably under the restraint of my pants. With my other hand, I pulled down the zipper and slipped my hand under my underwear, capturing myself in my hand. The feeling of suppressed desire made another moan slip out of me as I clenched my tip in my hand. "Daddy!" The way he cried that out was so sexy, my heart pounded as I replayed it over and over again as I ran my cupped hand over my dick up and down. Quickly wanting to find that release that I've been aching for.

His moans and...pleads for something more that not ever he understands. My index finger brushed over my tip, and not being able to hold it in anymore I rocked my hips against my hand while licking my lips. I let out a long moan as my head hit the back of my seat. My essence flew out in squirts staining the front of my pants as I panted. Now, that I had a taste of Lark I wasn't going to let him go anytime soon. I swore to that idiot father of his, that I was going to get a hold of that boy one way or another. He was going to be my baby, and I his daddy. Just the thought of that, had my balls clenching and whining for someone to touch them but I resisted. The day, that Lark willingly comes to me...there will be more of that. I grabbed a couple of tissues and wiped off the cum off of my now limp cock and pants and threw it out the window. My hand jobs weren't enough to satisfy me anymore, nothing made my blood roar the way it did with Lark-kun.

The static on the radio crackled as my fellow officers tried to communicate on the other side. To my annoyance, the door on my right opened suddenly as my parter Takashi slid in with two orders of coffees and fresh donuts. I glared at him from the side as he rubbed his hands together excitedly and started popping a donut into his mouth. "Really? You're a vampire who's primary food source is blood, and yet you eat human food." I scolded.

"You can have one if you want you know." I rolled my eyes as I put my seat belt on, and placed the car in drive and headed off back into our office. "Are you still thinking about that Lark-kun?" He said while trying to choke back a laugh, I clenched my hands around the steering wheel as he continued wheezing through the powdery sugared thing. "You really need a new sub, Tanaka. Lark-kun is straight remember? He told you himself."

"He's not entirely straight, I tasted his cum the other night and I know he liked it." I told him, watching in satisfaction as he coughed and nearly choked on that venom. "What!?"

"Its like I said..."

"I know what you said, Tanaka! But how, did you force him?"

"Nothing of that sort...I simply, snuck into his bedroom and gave him a taste of what it would be like to have me as a daddy."

"You are fucked up in the head Tanaka....his father will have your head for that!"

"Nevermind his father, if Lark-kun wants me away from him I will be. But as long as he wants me, there's no way I'll be leaving his side." Takashi rolled his eyes as we pulled up to the office near by, and I couldn't help but be surprised at the first person I would least expect to see, it was Lark himself. I put the car in park, watching with careful eyes as to why and how he was doing here.

Lark

What was I doing here? I told myself a thousand times, as I carefully stood in the police station of Sapparo, Japan. Oh yeah, the plan to seduce Tanaka

Raizo. After Dean and his small pack of wolves took me in that night we carefully went over the plan, I was supposed to kill a vampire. Since I was the only one that was able to get close enough to him in the first place. At first, Dean didn't approve of my seduction and neither did I. The plan was to get him as close to me as possible, and when it was time I would kill him. Nobody specified as to how long the seduction was to be, and I couldn't help but be worried about it.

Here I was, an average high school student trying to pull of C's in class now trying to seduce a vampire. But like Dean and my dad, they both wanted him dead. The thing was...I really didn't want to murder Tanaka and for some reason, I couldn't pin point the reason why. I don't know why, but...my mind always would trail back to the way he touched me that night. And my body secretly craved it, and wanted more of his touch. Is that normal? Especially when you're supposed to be mates with Dean? Why didn't I feel the same sexual attraction to Dean as I felt with Tanaka? We are mates aren't we? The door to the Sapporo police station opened and for some reason, I didn't need to turn around to know who it was, it was like my body knew on its own already.

"The man you want to see is here..." One of the cops who helped me out earlier said and made me jump a little clumsily as I turned around and faced him. His eyes met mine, and I gulped trying to still my beating heart as our eyes meet and stared at each other far longer than necessary. I was supposed to seduce him...but, it looked like he was the one that was going to seduce me instead. I already knew, how I was going to do it. I thought about it day and night since Dean, his pack and I talked. I just didn't know if I was able to put up with the plan or not.

"Lark-kun, what a surprise...." he said with a smirk as another cop beside him started laughing as he looked at us. I jumped at his laugh the laugh sounded like it was belittling me. But I ignored it as I came here only for one affirmative reason. "Come, we need privacy." Tanaka said as he nodded his head to the side as he walked me out of the Sapporo station and behind the building to the police station. Maybe this was a bad idea after all, maybe I should have talked this over with Dean or father but...if it was the only way to get close to him it was something that I was going to have to do.

"I find it interesting how you've managed to escape your people to come see me today. What brings you here Lark? Though I don't mind your presence really." Tanaka said while leaning against the side of the wall, the sounds of Sapporo city echoing around us. I tried to swallow my nerves down as my hands shook....

"I wanted to tell you something." I said, hating the way my voice shook as he stared at me. "Yes?"

"I...I agree to the contract." His eyes widened as he pushed himself away from the wall, not believing what he was hearing. "I'm sorry? I don't believe I heard you correctly...." He said while sauntering forward, so close that when my back hit the wall he caged me in with his arms on either side of me. Just...like the night before, I closed my eyes as my heart started pounding at him being so close. This may be the stupidest thing I have ever done, but....

"I want you to be my daddy." I whispered, feeling embarrassment sweep into my veins. "Look at me Lark-kun." I slowly peered my eyes open and body stared at him.

"Your father won't agree to this..." He purred as he he leaned down and his nose skimmed my neck making my breathing hitch.

"I don't care." I bit out...this was all part of the plan, I said as I tried to convince myself.

"Dean wouldn't approve." His nose skimmed up to my ear before taking my ear lobe into his mouth and sucking it, I let out a gasp at that.

"I-I d-don't care." I tried to sound as convincing as I possibly could, but his touch was making me weak in the knees, I used to be so sure...so certain that I wasn't gay, but the way this man touched me made my limbs turn into jelly and me feel something different. He made me feel hot. "You know what I am by now don't you?" He growled while grabbing my hips and pushing it towards his center. I gasped even more when I felt his bulge strain against my own bulge. "Y-yes..."

"You know why, your father and your own 'mate' wants you to be away from me so badly, and yet you still want me." He growled as he started grinding into me, making low whimpering sounds and other weird sounds come out of my mouth.

"Good." He growled as his mouth suddenly attacked my own in feverish kisses, I gasped hoarsely into his mouth as he pushed me against the wall and tugged his own pants down and tried to take off mine. "Take them of f..." he growled as he stopped kissing me. I did as he said without thinking, and he licked his lips as he yanked my underwear down forcibly. His touch was nothing like Dean's...no one made me feel the way he did like how he was doing. I gasped when he took off my shirt, leaving me stark naked in the back of a police station?

"Wait...wait!" I gasped as his mouth went down on one of my nipples and started licking and nipping at it while his other hand played with the other.

"This is a police s-station!" I gasped out loud when his cock suddenly rubbed against mine, over and over again, it was to the point where he left my hips shaking and quivering. His body completely covered mine as he looked into my eyes so intently that it almost made me want to cum right there.

"The-y c-an s-ee us." I panted as he leaned down and started placing feather like kisses against my neck. He rolled his hips as he continued grinding my dick with his, it almost felt like our dicks where dancing with each other.

"No....just relax baby." He moaned as he licked my neck again making my eyes roll back into my skull and my nipples hardening as the wind touched them. My head hit the back of the wall, the more his dick grinder against my own. This felt so good, "daddy...please." I moaned as I begged for that release that I wanted so badly. Tanaka let out a low, deep and throaty chuckle "damn baby. Don't know how you did it to escape your people or your father just to come and fuck..." I let out a moan as his touch sent sparks and tingles all over my body. My vision clouded into a haze of lust the more he grinned against my hardened dick.

"You want to feel my dick baby?" Tanaka whispered hoarsely into my ear making me whimper.

"Feels just like mine...just like mine." I whimpered as his hand kept brushing my nipple and it was then that I couldn't take the pleasure anymore and let myself cum.

"Call me daddy baby..."

"Daddy!" I cried out as I came, his dick stopped grinding and soon after I felt his essence drip all over onto my own dick, our cum mixing together.

"So fucking hot baby...." My hooded eyes started blinking in and out of focus as we both panted as we reluctantly parted away from each other and started getting dressed. For some reason, my body still wanted more, and my dick still strained against my jeans. Tanaka's eyes suddenly turned red as he brought me into his chest.

"Tell me baby...who do you belong to?"

"You Tanaka only you." I said without thinking, as he hummed and placed a finger under my chin and made me look at him as he smirked in satisfaction at my response. And then, I went limp in his arms.

Never Let Go

A/N: Sorry for the wait! Enjoy the chapter! Things are going to take an interesting turn from here. Poor Dean.

I tried reminding myself that it was all part of the plan.

Tanaka and I were in his apartment that day as he brought me the contract that I needed to sign. The lights were dim in his apartment as we sat around his coffee table. He gave me a bottle of water and I couldn't help but notice that he wasn't drinking anything. We were talking about all the possibilities about this type of relationship. That is, if you can even call it a relationship, a fake relationship sounded just about right to me. As each hour passed, we carefully went over the different types of arrangements that can be made. And the little parts of the contracts to.

The contract was 11 pages long.

We went over every page line by line, and he made sure that I understood everything. I was supposed to kill him with dragon glass, bring an end to the race of rogue vampires. The ones who feed off the blood of the innocents. I reminded myself that I'm supposed to be the heir of the hunting clan. A clan that my father worked so hard building for, that it got to where it was today.

Just as I was about to sign the last page, confirming the contract and its explicitations Tanaka's hand reached over and grabbed my wrist. My eyes swept up to his body over me, "before you sign that, I just want to know...are you aware of what I am?" He asked while licking his lips, I tried swallowing my dry throat feeling my tongue get scrambled up so I just nodded. Tanaka raised his brows in surprise at my response.

"I want you to say it....say what I am out loud." He whispered.

"A vampire." I whispered softly. "I'm not afraid of you." I responded, knowing that despite him being a vampire I know he wouldn't do anything to me, but, I'm afraid of what I could to him. I'm just a human, an amateur even that was supposed to kill him. I haven't killed anyone before in my life. The thought of that plays over and over in my mind as I sat across from him. "I can hear that you're lying to me Lark-kun, your heart skips a beat when that happens. But its normal to be afraid, when you're surrounded by werewolves who tell you nothing but negative truths about our existence."

If only he knew what I was really afraid of, I'm glad that vampires can't read minds.

"If only you knew what us vampires say about werewolf." He teased, causing me to smirk a little bit.

"I bet...you say a lot of negative truths about them." I shrugged my shoulders as he chuckled, he leaned back and sunk into the wooden chair. And handed me the pen again, I grabbed it and without thinking signed my name in a crappy looking cursive design. Officially sealing the deal, I set the pen aside and slid the contract over to Tanaka who had the biggest smile on his face that I've ever seen. Who would've known that signing one contract could make someone so happy. It was painfully ironic. I gulped, hooking my index finger around my collar and stretching it outwards.

"I'm glad we got that out of the way." He said as he put the contract away in a near by briefcase. And it was then that I had to ask him if he had other subs before..."h-have...you had..." I shook my head, I couldn't finish that sentence. Tanaka raised a perfect eyebrow and leaned forward with his hands neatly folded, and tucked underneath his chin. "Have I had what Lark-kun? Others before you? Other subs? If that is what you mean to ask, then yes I have." I gulped, I was right Tanaka was clearly a man of sexual experience. And then here I was in front of him, a guy who once thought he was straight and is on the verge of understanding or coming to terms with being gay.

"Why me then? Why not just have another vampire sub with more experience then me?" I asked exasperatedly. "Why not you?" Tanaka fired back, almost as if he was offended by my question. "You're perfect." I rolled my eyes, "anything but that." It was quite for awhile as we sat there looking at each other with blank looks on our faces, so now it was official. Now, I'm his sub, just like he wanted. And now, I had the opportunity to do what I came for, but could I really do it?

"So, where does this start?"

"We have a relationship, just as normally as a male and female couple would my dear Lark-kun." He chuckled making my cheeks flush red in embarasment.

"Okay." I told him.

"But for now, I would like to introduce you to other dominants and subs to make you feel more comfortable in this type of world." He mentioned carefully as if silently asking me for my permission with his eyes.

"Other dominants? Subs?" I asked."In a relationship such as this one, dominants are usually the one in control when it comes to what happens in between the sheets." My face turned scarlet at that.

"And subs are...""I think I get the main idea." I whispered, looking down at the table feeling myself grow shy.

It was a comfortable kind of silence for awhile. The same type of silence that I felt when we walked in the park filled of cherry blossom trees. I didn't understand, but I felt more at ease with Tanaka than I did with Dean. Even if Dean is supposedly my mate.

"Does your father know where you are?" He asked, I shook my head subtly. "Does Dean?" Again, I shook my head.

"I see." He hummed while getting out of his chair and making a phone call.After a few minutes, he turned off his phone, and tucked it back into his front pocket.

"Well, its about to turn dark..." He said while looking out in a nearby window. "Come, I want to introduce you to the others."

I gulped, as realization dawned on me...I just signed my soul to the devil.

Tanaka was already making his way toward the front door of his apartment as he waited for me. I followed him slowly, debating on wether or not I should call Dean. But I did leave him a note explaining my absence, hoping that he understood.

I slipped into the car seat next to him on the left hand side and strapped in my seatbelt. I should have felt scared, but I don't.

Tanaka turned the engine on as we sped off in the middle of the night. We were surrounded by flashing lights overhead. And my eyes couldn't help but widen on their own as my senses became overwhelmed.

Japan came alive at night.

There wee so many sights to see and explore. I couldn't help but point to each building excitedly and show Tanaka. He smiled as if he were enjoying my excitement. And when we turned left, and slowed down to a stop. I couldnt help but feel saddened that all the sight seeing was over.

"Do not worry Lark, we have all the time in the world to take a look at Japan." I blushed when he smiled at me again. He parallel parked perfectly on the side of the curb and once he got out he opened the door for me.

"Thanks."

The city streets of Japan were filled with life as my senses became overwhelmed. The sound of the city made the blood flow in my veins, I was afraid of getting lost almost. But Tanaka kept a good grip on my left hand and guided me through the sea of people.

"Where are we going!?" I shouted throughout the noise around us.

"A club!" He replied, as we passed through a couple mode blocks and finally in the dark corner we found a huge line of people wearing revealing clothing. Some had every inch of them tattooed.My eyes widened when a lot of them looked at me curiously, but when they looked at Tanaka. They looked away.

Could they tell that I was human? How did I smell like to them? As if sensing my uncomfortable state, Tanaka pulled me closer to his side as he walked up to a big looking guy at the front door.

"Tanaka! Good to see you again." He came here often?

"Likewise."

"So, you brought another one of them this time?" He chuckled as he looked down at me. "He's the one, he signed the contract a few hours ago." Tanaka said with a proud looking smile on his face.

"Well then, welcome." He said to Tanaka at first and gave me a sideways glance. I blushed when his stare was a lot longer than normal. And at that idea, Tanaka took me away from him and brought me into the club.

My jaw dropped at the lights, the moving bodies grinding against ea-chother. Some people were even making out in a corner. I looked away from them as my shyness over my virginity swept over me.Here, I was, a virgin in the middle of a room full of horny vampires.

I adjusted my collar as Tanaka lead me into the a table full of vampires. He was leading me in a pit of snakes. I could instinctively feel the panic begin to swell in me as Tanaka pulled me close. His breath tickled my ear as he assured me that nothing was going to happen.As we approached the table, a familiar face was on a larger guy's lap with bulging muscles. It was the guy from school, Hajime!

A furious blush swept across my cheeks, as I took in the compromising position that he was in. It looked like he was really enjoying himself, being shameless in front of the group of men who acted like nothing was happening before their very eyes. As if sensing my unease, Tanaka leaned down and smiled at me. "That behavior is normal around here for doms and their subs." He chuckled as he sat down on the love seat, and pulled me onto his lap. I blushed as all of a sudden the attention was turned onto me. The Dom's arms around Hajimie's waist stilled as if he sensed my presence and made Hajime turn around, but kept him in his lap.

Holy cow! The guy was ripped, and he was shirtless.

Tanaka's hand gripped my waist, as Hajime finally saw me. "Lark-kun! Its so good to see you again, and I'm surprised at such circumstances too!" He said excitedly, and then turned to Tanaka. "Did he finally agree to be your sub?"

"Yes." Tanaka said while puffing out his chest, as though he were proud of it, proud of me. But why? I had nothing to be prideful of, I was just a short and skinny guy who wasn't that smart. But still got around.

"Interesting." My eyes swept over to the shirtless guy, "a human for a sub, is he that good in bed Raizo?"

A small growl ripped from Tanaka's mouth as he held me protectively in front of him.

"Perhaps, we could share him one day." I didn't like where this was going anymore, he was one of those guys to be on the look out for. "Watch who you're talking to Takumi." A slow smirk spread on his face, and I couldn't help but notice the dejected look on Hajime's face. Did that guy flirt with other subs in front of him all the time? A frown formed on my face at the thought of it. I was hoping, that he would stay away from me. I didn't want anything to sabotage our friendship. I couldn't help but notice that he was wearing some kind of pretty looking collar around his neck.

"Why so possessive Tanaka? Its not like you gave him a collar yet, if he has no collar he is free."

"I would shut that hole in your face, Takumi you know how Tanaka gets." A new voice popped out from the crowd as I felt the pumping vibrations of the music touch the table.

"I'm just playing, we all know that." Takumi chuckled as Tanaka gripped my hand, got up from the table and lead me to the dance floor. That wasn't a really good idea, I'm not that great of a dancer.

"Ooooo dancing! I love to dance, take me to the dance floor Takumi please." I heard Hajime whine as my head looked over my shoulder. The rest of the conversation grew distant as a hoard of horny people started grinding against each other when the music changed to a more rythymnous beat. People tried grinding on me, but Tanaka pulled me closer to his body, leaving no room or space. It started getting really heated in here. "Maybe it was a mistake bringing you here, in a room full of vampires." He shouted against my ear as he started moving us two and fro to the music. I shook my head, in disagreement.

And Tanaka stopped talking. He moved my hips against hips, rocking it in tune to the pace of the music. "I can't dance!" I shouted, trying to push myself away from him but instead he latched on, and that was when I felt it. Something large and huge brushed against me bum as he turned me around and pulled me up against him.

"Grind..." He whispered hotly against my ear lobe. "Feel the music." He whispered again, as he pushed my hips back against his bulge. "Feel me." He said as he took my earlobe into his mouth and started nipping against it. I let out a surprised gasp at the soft contact, but did as he said and with no questions asked. I let my mind slip away and let my body grind against him as he held my hips and moved them against his groin. I couldn't help but let out a small breathy moan when his lips made contact with my neck, he was leaving small butterfly kisses up and down my neck. And they stopped when they reached a certain spot that sent a jolt of electricity and sparks all around my body. I gasped, arching my neck and letting my neck fall against the base of his shoulder.

Something sharp pricked my neck, and at the dull pain my eyes widened at the realization of what he was doing! I stopped grinding, and paused to see if anyone noticed but everyone was all lost in their own world and I tried pulling myself away even more but he grasped on. The pain was there, I whimpered when I felt his sharp fangs elongate and prick the sensitive flesh of my neck. I thrashed a bit, but he shushed me against my neck. The pain lasted for a few minutes, it felt like you were getting your blood drawn for testing at the hospital. But then, I didn't know what it was but something felt really really good.

I let out a moan as I felt his fangs sink deeper into my neck, and felt my own groin throb with heat. My pants felt uncomfortable as Tanaka started encouraging me to grind against me as the music changed into a rougher beat. "T-Tanaka..." I felt embarrassed when I moaned out his name as he started sucking my blood. Then, those delicious sparks stopped as I felt him pull out his fangs my neck.

"You taste, so good. I'm never going to let you go Lark-kun."

Chapter 19

A/N: Soooo sorry, for this super late update! I'm in my second to my last semester in college right now, and things are piling up for me. I was finally able to write something today though! Yay!

The music was pounding hard and loud against my ear drums, I couldn't feel or hear anything save for my own heartbeat as Tanaka boldy echoed those words of firey passion against my ears. He still held my body against his chest as a swarm of people started grinding against each other, it felt like we were the only people in the world as we stood in the middle of the dance floor. Did anyone see what just happened between us? A wave of embarrassment washed over me, as Tanaka still held on to me pressing butterfly kisses to my neck every now and then. And, despite my embarrassment, I still felt aroused.

Why was I feeling this way towards Tanaka all of a sudden? Wasn't Dean supposed to be my mate in the first place? Wasn't I supposed to feel this type of attraction to Dean only?? I felt conscious at the fact that we were behaving so openly in a crowded room full of horny vampires. I tried to step away from him because I didn't want this to get too far, too soon. But instead of letting me go, just like he promised he grabbed my waist and held my body firmly against his broad and muscled chest. I had to surpres an embarrassing moan when I felt his own arousal bump against the back of my thighs.

Dean was suddenly long gone from my mind.

I felt every kiss that went up my neck to the bone, until all of a sudden, he took my earlobe in his mouth and nibbled on it, making me shiver until he whispered in my ear "where do you think you're going?" He said, his voice dipping an octave lower than before making me shiver as my eyes hazed.

"You like that?" I shivered when he dipped my ear lob into his mouth. I can not believe that he was nibbling my ear. I heard about this experience a lot in maybe I don't know yaoi fanfiction? But now that it was happening to me it felt really weird and a little uncomfortable. I tensed up a bit but then all of a sudden what I felt before was washed away as his tongue flicked a certain part of a ear lobe and I couldn't help an embarrassing sound that came out of my mouth. Tanaka chuckled hoarsely and stopped doing what was he was doing and stepped away from my body.

"We can't do this here." I panted out as I tried to pull away from him but again he grabbed onto my wrist and laugh of course he would. I should learn by now from him.

"You're right." He whispered, I widened my eyes at that, "huh?" I asked him dumbly. "We should do this back at my apartment.

Wow, that suddenly took a drastic turn more than I expected really. A thought suddenly came to my mind, "wait, wait!" I told him suddenly feeling shy and a little panicky at the thought of what we were about to do in his apartment. He arched a brow, "yes?" I'm still shocked at the fact that I can even hear Tanaka over the vibration of music that is pounding vigorously around us. I gulped and played with my fingers a bit, "I need to make a phone call." I told him, unsure if he was willing to let me go even if twas just for a few minutes. I needed to call my dad and let him know that I was okay, after all I did leave without a warning and for more than a couple of days. Only Dean and their pack knew where the bloody heck I was at this point.

Tanaka body froze, as though he were a little uncertain as to letting me make that call. I gulped and felt my throat grow dry as cotton at his pause, but to my surprise and surge of relief he let me make that call.

"Alright." He said with a firm nod, but still seemed hesitant.

"We'll head out together so that you can make that call outside, there's no way I'm leaving you alone in coven full of vampires waiting to suck your delicious blood." My eyes widened at that and he just started laughing at my reaction.

"Come on my Lark-kun, we're leaving early." He took me by the hand and carefully led me out of the dancing bodies that were trying to grind on us even on our way out! Tanaka kept me close to him and this time I didn't mind it because I didn't want some stranger to start groping me out of the blue and for no reason. Well, it wouldn't really be for no reason because I am not that bad looking after all. As Tanaka checked us out of the club and the pounding of the music was there only faintly behind us as the darkness swallowed up the building around us. I let out a breath of relief at thought of being less suffocated around a bunch of vampires. That was not a place I really wanted to be. The only vampire that I wanted to be around was Tanaka. I shivered at the thought, making Tanaka stop in his step a few cars away from his own.

"Why are we stopping?" Tanaka didn't say anything at first, only puckered his lips before pulling off his sexy leather jacket and slipping it around me. Inside, I couldn't help but melt a little bit.

"You are cold, no?" He asked linking his hand with mind as he took out his car keys and the sound of the beep to open the car was heard.

"What about you?" I asked him, who started barking out a laugh, he took a hold of my hand and stared at me "do I feel cold to you? Do you think I'm that Edward guy from Twilight you Americans are so fond of?" I blushed and his hand was not skin cold, it warm really warm.

"You're hot." I said with my eyes widening never paying attention to it before, no wonder my own pulse was rising when I was so close to him and felt my body heat up before.

"Thank you Lark, you're adorable."

My face sputtered in embarrassment at that..."I-I...I...." Tanaka rolled his eyes and let out a sigh. "I'm going to have fun with you Lark."

Yeah, sure...

"Wait, Tanaka...the call?" He arched a brow, if it is that important to you surely you wouldn't mind making that call when you are safe with me in the car now would you?" I gulped and shrugged my shoulders, suddenly not feeling the urge to call anybody anymore. I sucked up what pride I had left and let my body open the door and slide to the car seat next to him. I gulped and sat in silence in the car ride back to his apartment. I didn't know what was going to happen the moment we go back , and it didn't help that the car ride to the club and back was only for 25 minutes from where he lived.

"What's on your mind Lark?" He asked as he looked straight ahead still at the strangely small amount of traffic.

"N-nothing." I gulped, damn, I really hated it when I stuttered when I'm nervous.

"Weren't you going to make that call?" He asked suddenly sounding very curious, as I tried to find a way to feign a reason.

"I uh...its okay I changed my mind."

"Interesting, how you changed your mind on such a last minute notice my Lark-kun...." He whispered but then all of a sudden I let out a gasp when he made a sharp turn around the corner and before I knew it we were already in front of his apartment. Damn vampires and their speed. I gulped, at Tanaka's sudden change of mood was he going to do something to me? The door on my right unlocked and he encouraged me to get out on my own which I gladly obliged to. Tanaka was an unpredictable person, and I'm not sure if that's a good thing or not with him at this point. As we made our way up the staircase, I silently watched him open the door to his apartment and slowly followed him behind.

This was going to be a long night.

The Vampire Coven Part 1

As we went up the stairs to his apartment my heart couldn't stop beating....could he hear that? I couldn't help but think that as a vampire, does he have heightened senses like the werewolves? What does my blood smell like to him? "Welcome to my humble abode, Lark-kun" my bead snapped up to the sound of his voice as he encouraged me to walk into his apartment. I did, but slowly and hesitantly, after all I was walking into a vampire's home.

"Uhm, thanks..." I squeeked but then managed to clear my throat."Do you want anything to drink or eat?" He asked me but I shook my head in a silent no thank you. Tanaka seemed dissatisfied with that but let it go. He was about to say something else when his phone started to ring.

"Pardon me, this will take a moment to answer." Tanaka said as he slowly left the room, I took a minute or two to take a glance at my surroundings. Tanaka was clearly a simple but orderly for a vampire. I dared to move myself around the free dark space. How was I ever going to commit myself to killing a man that I was starting to have unwanted feelings for? I was supposed to be mated to Dean right?

When Tanaka left the room, I took that as my cue to begin exploring his apartment. Could Tanaka be the one that is killing all those victims in Japan? I started by taking off in the small kitchen nearby, I was sure that he wouldn't mind if I went for a drink right? I opened the front door of the refrigerator and fell to the floor wincing when I broke something sharp behind me. His whole refrigerator was filled with labeled blood bags. Everywhere I looked it was filled, my eyes went wide as saucers and I struggled to get up when he called out to me.

"Lark is everything alright? I heard something break!" I jumped up clumsily from my crouched position on the floor and closed the door while making a lame attempt at trying to pick up the pieces of broken glass. "Y-yeah.. .ev-erything is f-fine!" I stuttered but winced when a piece of glass broke into my skin. "Ouch..." I hissed peering down at the small drop of blood that was oozing out of my skin. In a blink of an eye, Tanaka suddenly appeared...and his eyes were instantly focused on my blood. Rather than the mess on the floor.

My heart was beating hard and fast inside of my chest, as I tried to back away from the now hungry vampire in front of me. But, in a speed that I've never knew that he possessed. He was in front of me. "I'm s-sorry about the mess I'll clean it up." I promised him, as nerves made my voice quiver. Then I started babbling, I would always babble whenever I'm nervous.

"I--" He suddenly shushed me quietly while getting the items that I dropped on the floor picked up.

"It's okay Lark kun we all make mistakes from time to time." He mused as he bent over to clean everything. As he did though, I couldn't help but notice that this was my chance to kill him. I kept the dagger close to my jacket and slowly reached in in order to pull it out. I gulped as my hands began to shake as I held it high with both of my hands. But then Tanaka stopped cleaning and when I tried to dig in the dagger into his back he was much quicker than I was. I gasped when he straightened up and quickly grabbed my wrist just seconds away from hitting his back. I froze at his touch, while he tsked.

"Lark, Lark, Lark..." You really do not want to be doing what you're about to do. He grabbed the dagger out of my hands and took a look at it underneath a lamp.

"Your werewolfs honestly think that this can kill a vampire? We're immortals for a reason Lark."

"I would tell you the only way for you to kill me but...you'll just try that on your own won't you?" Tanaka smiled, but I couldn't help but shake as nerves filled my every being. He was a vampire, who could easily kill me now that he caught a human almost trying to kill me. How can I face Dean and the others now? I really didn't plan this out.

What do I say to that I'm sorry? Me and my nervous self can't bring ourselves to do that.

Instead, I stuttered. "I--I..." I have to get out of here, I realized or he'll end up killing me like his other victims.

"I know you're sorry about the incident, and you really didn't mean to kill me Lark."

Huh?

"I'm willing to imagine that you really didn't want to kill me and that you were put up with it is that right?" I gulped and shakily shook my head yes. It was like I was in a trance, and I felt compelled to just agree with everything he said.

"Good Lark. I can forgive you for this knowing that killing me wasn't truly your intention at all. However, you must be willing to pay back the damage you've cost." I leaned over as pointed out the mess that was now sprawled unto the floor.

"I'm sorry..." I finally managed to whisper when he leaned me against one of the wooden cabinets of the kitchen.

"Are you really now?" He whispered as he leaned closer to me, almost hovering me. But it was as if time suddenly froze and stopped when my ringtone on my back pocket began to go off. Please don't be them, I begged watching him as he slowly arched an eyebrow but then he let out an eerily small smile street his face as he reached back and gently cupped my bottom. I gasped at the unexpected touch and froze as I felt his hand run over my but cheek felt him pull out my phone.

Shit.

He flipped it open and answered the call.

"Hello?" He asked keeping one of his muscled arms on the other side of me. Tanaka looked at me curiously and smirked deviously when he put the phone on speaker.

"Lark? Where are you are you alright! Who are you you bastard! What did you do to him?" Dad! I gasped.

"Where are you Lark?"

"Your son is alright and safe with me." Tanaka chuckled.

"Son, we'll find you...wherever you are you hear me?" Tanaka turned off the phone and put it into his own back pocket.

My heart started racing a mile a minute, and I know that he heard it. He's a vampire, vampires have heightened senses compared to a human's.

"I must say that I'm disappointed Lark...that you would still be afraid of me even after all this time." I stood against the cabinet not being able to control my shaking body of course, while I can't deny being attracted to a vampire. His unpredictability is what scared me the most about him.

"A-are you the one thats been killing all of the victims in Japan?" I found myself asking."No." He said after a pregnant pause.

"He is still being tracked down by my coven. When I do my feeding I'm always sure to be careful." He said with a frown."Your father and your so call mate Dean will surely be looking for you soon, I will need to take you home soon." Home? As in to his little bat cave? And meet his other vampire friends?

"Don't you worry Lark-kun, daddy will be sure to take care of his baby."I suddenly wished that I never moved to Japan.

A/N: Sorry for the late update, I should be able to update the next one sometime this week. comments=love :).

The Vampire Coven Part 2

A/N: YES!!! I is back! Helloooo my friends, I'm sorry for the late update I've been really stressed out with reality. So I'm back! I put on my writing goggles and zoomed back into wattpad. Sorry for the hiatus. I had family problems, a lot of fighting going on in my extended family. And then the real world on my own stopped me from figuring out what to write about. And I almost lost a sense of writing because of stress. But it's all good now, and I hope you enjoy the new chapter of "The Hunt!" ^.^

Something was really wrong in this neighborhood.

Raw animal instinct took over. Once human, and innocent. The animal in Tanaka came to life.

Like a moth to flame, Tanaka crossed the loft in three broad strides and fell to his knees at the girl's back. His black hair framing his face. Long nose, and a blue marking on his right arm. He pulled his kerchief down—he needed every drop of her scent.

He realizes.

In order to track a human. He needed her scent, her blood.

A wolf smelt different then a human. A wolf, those beasts, smelt like sulfur.

A human, like raw fish.

He took his hat off too, set it behind him on a nearby bale. Then he scooped her fiery curls in one handful, pressed them to his face, and breathed in deep.

Delicious. He thought to himself.

What would her blood taste like if he took just one bite off of her skin?

He exhaled a soft small growl.

Mine.

Inwardly, he felt his eyes flash and change.

And he automatically felt territorial to what belonged to him. The only words that flew across his mind were these:

" A mate is someone that belongs to them. It's there's and only theirs. And anything that shall be learnt from them will come from their dominant."

Was the only word that swept through his mind as he put his pushed his mate aside for later. Tanaka paced the loft of his dark apartment that only consisted of his desk and a few lamps, a sofa, and a T.V. set. And ran a shaky palm through his hair. He was upset, there was no way there was no way that his Lark had two mates. Lark belonged to him. And only him. At the thought, he snapped and rushed towards his mate and wrapped a palm over his frail shoulder and lowered his ear to his mouth. He felt slow, wispy and shakey breath. Surely, Lark was intimidated by his closeness as Tanaka's vampire senses picked up a fluttering pulse. Alive. Good. Asleep, or knocked out cold. It didn't matter, because once Tanaka was already down there, his good cheek hovering over her high, lacy neckline, instinct raged.

Whether this stubborn boy admitted it or not, Lark is attracted to him.

He pressed Lark onto his back and was over him in an instant, straddling him. This little peach blossom was his, all his. He wanted to devour, but before you devoured, you had to prune. Sandor needed his peach to be pretty. He needed him to be safe.

He had a set of scratches along his jaw. A couple more on his hands. His dress was rumpled, stained with mud at the hem. But no blood. No bones at odd angles. And most importantly—no bite. Sandor pried him collar down with a finger to check. All clear.

His little boy was unclaimed. He would have to change that.

So Tanaka decided to clean him up. He licked the patches of dirt from his full, rosy cheeks, fevered beneath his tongue. He nursed the scratches on his jaw, scabbed, healing. Good.

He opened his mouth wide over Lark's bare neck. He set his teeth there. He even let them sink into her tender, yielding flesh, but just a little. Gods, he wanted him. His nether regions stirred in his pants. And he wanted a bite of this ripe peach. But he hesitated—slobber spilled from his maw and dripped down into the girl's hair. He couldn't bring his teeth down, to part his pulp. He closed up.

Tanaka put his cheek to his neck instead, and basked in his puddle of spit. Oh Gods, it was good. After he laid his scent there, he worked his way down, over a stiff bodice that trapped two tender budding nipples. Sucking them there. Tanaka swirled his good cheek on those too, marveling at the boy's softness. He would have put his scars on him—they weren't hurting so much with her scent in his nose—but they might have cracked during the ride. He didn't want to get blood on her pretty dress. Lark wore fine satin, his peach. It covered his arms and down to his little leather boots.

Tanaka went lower, yes sir. He buried his nose in Lark's cute little belly. His feeble breath coming out in soft breaths, as he pushed him back; he liked that. What he liked more was thinking of a bigger belly. He pictured his small peach stuffed with fresh cream. Seed taking root, sprouting. He smelled perfect. Tanaka smelled strength on him. He could take him, every inch. The knot, too.

Lark's small groan undid him. He wasn't sure if he was actually going to hoist those shiny jeans and stick himself inside her, but he didn't get the chance. He brought his nose down to the mound between his legs, cloaked in dampened fabric. He was thinking of juicy red fruit. He was thinking of a hard pit in the center. He took Lark's small hips in his hands, drank his scent in belly-deep.

His cock lunged and pulsed, as he unleashed a groan into folds of his wardrobe.

The boy moaned at Tanaka's touch.

He had to stop himself.

He couldn't hurt him. Tanaka thought, as a sob left his lips at the corner of the bed. His shoulder shaking.

He was horny.

But he couldn't do it. He couldn't hurt him. Something in him stopped him from hurting the boy.

Fair. But Tanaka hated the sound, and he especially hated how his wide eyes pooled with tears. They spilled down his flushed cheeks, then the sobs started. Lark tried to scramble backwards, as fear overtook him but he wasn't going anywhere with Tanaka's fingers sunk into her hips. So he tried throwing straw at him instead, pitiful handfuls that only served to dirty him.

Tanaka got tired of the struggle. He trapped his wrists in his hands and yanked her up until their noses touched. "Stop," he growled into Lark's trembling lips.

Lark surrendered of course. But then he started again and It was far worse.

Tanaka knew that look all too well. He'd be hard-pressed to find someone who didn't give him that look. The human was done sobbing, but he cried. Pretty, sparkling tears fell from her eyes as they searched his scars. Tanaka had found himself a peach. He had found a beast. A shit trade, that. Tanaka's gut turned to cold stone. He let go of his wrists. He dropped back to the bale where he had left his hat, and put it right back on. He made sure his hair was plastered to the bad side of his face.

The boy, believe or not, lifted his wrists to her nose. He breathed in, and his face twisted. His thighs shifted beneath his clothes, and he mashed a palm down between them. When Lark looked back up, she was frowning.

"It's you," he breathed.

"It's me," Tanaka replied. Knowing that Lark finally recognized him as his mate.

"But you're—you're—"

"Ugly. I know." He responded.

The boy whimpered in fear. It was a pathetic noise, but Tanaka's cock liked the sound of it. He should take him—no one could stop him. Not Dean, or his parents. He wanted his damn pie, tears or no tears. He'd be wet no matter what. As if he heard him, his cries got loud again. He rubbed her eyes with her fists like a sad little pup and wailed, "It hurts."

Tanaka breathed out a growl. "Where?" he rasped.

Tanaka cleared up his throat with a cough, then spit a mouthful of peach pulp down to the barn floor. Splat. Better.

"Where's you my bird?" Tanaka asked through tight teeth.

"I'm not a bird," Lark said.

"Then how did you fly so far?"

The boy shook his head, sporting a true champion's pout. A sad little bird. Lonely, maybe. He curled back up again, wrapping his arms around his legs and dropping his head to his knees. "I'm Lark, not a bird." "And everything hurts. You made it hurt worse."

Tanaka hated the sound of that. "I'll make it better," he offered. He stuck out his hand to give him something to sniff. Almost forgetting that Lark was a human and not a vampire. But it did not matter it was instinct. The boy perked up, but didn't accept. So he tried his nice voice, his calming voice, the one the boys at his coven liked. "I know I'm scary, little bird. But I'm a good mate. I promise."

That got him to take his large hand. The bird he loved so much already held his palm face up, his little hands curled on either side of it. He lowered his nose, inhaled, then whimpered. "Please help me," he said.

"Can I touch?"

The boy nodded, even tugged Tanaka forward a bit. He put his legs aside hers, a big cage for a tiny bird. When he fumbled with his jeans, he whispered, "Don't look." As he looked away.

When his fingers landed on his dewy, inflamed flesh, his groan escaped. "Oh, little bird," he growled.

"What is it?" he peeped.

"You're swollen, bad. Are you alright? Do you hurt anywhere—"

Lark blushed like a damn girl. Thankfully, the boy shook her head at him, but she frowned again. "It's my first time," he quietly said.

"Not like this." Lark said as he caressed his head and moved his dark curls to a side. Allowing himself to feel the soft flesh on a hard pit. "Hold on tight," he told him.

It was a tricky business, climbing down the ladder one handed, backwards and blind, with a delicate creature on his hip, but Tanaka somehow seemed manage just fine. He found solid footing and navigated out from the barn to the cabin. He knew his way in the light of the waxing moon. He carried his bird up the rickety porch steps to the main room, and set her gently down in a chair by the hearth. He had to get the fire going right quick of course, so the girl didn't freeze.

After the kindling caught and Tanaka threw a couple logs on, he fetched the knit blanket he kept at the foot of his bed. Didn't warm him up none—it was Margaery's, from so long ago. A sentimental thing mostly. Lark looked real pretty in it. His hair mirrored the fire, and his cheeks glowed a full rosy red. She was smiling too, a sleepy smile. She aimed it straight at Sandor.

"Can I have some cake, please?" He asked.

Tanaka laughed. "You take me for a baker, is it? I haven't bought sugar my whole sorry life."

His smile disappeared in an instant. "I'll make you something sweet, little bird," Tanaka recovered instantly. He picked up Lark's face and brushed his thumb over his lips. "Don't you fret."

He didn't have sugar, but he had honey. Wildflower honey, from the market up in Hornvale. Liquid gold. He hooked the kettle over the hearth and got some winter wheat bubbling nicely. When the grains swelled and split, he stirred in a couple spoonfuls of honey. He was feeling particularly generous, so after he piled the porridge in a wooden bowl, he stuck a pat of butter right on top. A real treat.

His sweet peach liked it. Lark ate slowly, chewing and swallowing delicate bites like a proper lady. While she did that, Tanaka had his chance to tend to Stranger. He got his stallion undressed and cozied up in the stable for the night. He gave him an extra armful of hay for his good work during the drive, and of course he got a kiss good night. Damn good horse, that Stranger.

Lark followed Tanaka back inside the cabin like apartment. He immediately padded to Lark's side and pawed at his porridge. "Boy, down," Tanaka called out. Lark gave him an insolent look, then put a long lick across the boy's knuckles.

Lark giggled. "Lady, down," he mocked.

The bitch did as he was told at least. He sat on his fluffy behind and smiled so wide his tongue fell out. And Lark, the naughty little bird, set his bowl on the floor to feed Tanaka's dog his leftovers. When Tanaka noticed Lark's narrowed eyes, he smirked.

"I'm ready for bed," he told him, then stretched out his arms expectantly.

Lark was a smart bird, that's what. Tanaka came to him. He held his shoulders as he scooped Lark from the chair into his arms, still bundled in his little blanket. He was light as a peach blossom. It almost felt as if Tanaka carried nothing but sweet-smelling air down the hall. The boy was over him like a cloud. And before Tanaka knew, his soft little face nuzzled into his neck. His cold nose pressed right down on his patch of skin that stunk the most.

He'd never had a human scent him before. He liked it. He liked it a lot. It called the monster in him.

When he pushed open the door to his bedroom, Lark whimpered like she he in the loft and shrunk into him—his musk had rained down like a half ton of brick. "Too much?" Sandor asked. Lark nodded against his chest. "Alright. We'll do the other.

The other had been his room as a boy, his and Gregor's. It was empty now, except for a narrow pine bed with a leather bound chest at its foot. Sandor set the girl down on the edge of the bed, and she looked up at him, unblinking.

"My boots, please," he said, kicking out Lark's heels.

Tanaka grumbled, but knelt, and went to work unlacing Lark's dusty leather boots. They were small, fit for a doll. He winced when he tugged off the first one, so he went real slow with the next. When he rolled down her stockings, he realized why all the fuss—his little toes were covered in angry blisters.

"Oh, little bird," he breathed. He didn't know how to make this better. Nothing to do with blisters but wait them out. But the girl frowned down at him so hard, he knew he had to think of something. So he picked up her feet, both at once, and brought them to his mouth. They were funky little fruits, but he kissed them. Put lots of soft little kisses all over his toes, until he got a giggle out of her. He kissed harder, everywhere, down to her heels and up her ankles. He even licked her a bit, so he could hear more of Lark's pretty noises. He had started nipping at the ball of bone that stuck from her ankle when she batted the top of his hat and whined,

"Stop. I'm not dinner." Lark whimpered.

Tanaka was a good alpha, so he put his feet down. He pulled back the covers for her, and guided her head down to her pillow. As soon as he pulled the well-worn quilt to her chin, His little lady, Lark, hopped up and curled right beside her. Took up damn near half the mattress.

"Lark," Tanaka warned. But Lark hugged the dog, and let him lay dozens of sloppy kisses on his lips. Tanaka sighed. "Fine, he can stay. But if he starts to whine in his sleep, rub his belly. He likes that."

Lark nodded, and pressed his face into his black fur coat. Tanaka lingered beside the bed. He wanted the girl's face in his hair. He wanted to lick his lips clean of honey. He wanted to lick every pretty inch of her skin. It would be creamy, and smooth, and soft.

Imagine the taste.

"Are you going to watch me all night?" the boy mumbled, eyes shut.

Tanaka turned red. He was going to say something, really, but she went on, "It's alright if you do, but a chair would be more comfortable. Or maybe the floor, don't you think?"

Tanaka forced a crude breath through his nose, nostrils flared. The boy didn't spare him a glance. He was good at feigning sleep, or maybe she was that exhausted. So he stalked to the door—he was done with her spoiled antics, heat or no heat. But right before he stormed out, he looked back. What a sight, that sweet, fiery blossom snuggled up with his favorite gal. His heart did that thing again, stopping and thumping like a metronome awry. It felt off, but good at the same time. His lips twitched at the corner. He put a palm to his neck, right where the young boy's face had been.

"Good night, little peach," he grumbled to his boots, before leaving Lark in the dark.

Now, behind closed doors, his phone rang in his pocket. Tanaka shuffled the phone out of his pocket and pulled it out. Knowing there was no collar ID on it and answered the call.

"It's time." The voice hissed sharply on the other end of the line.

Tanaka gulped, his mouth dry like cotton, instantly missing the boy's warmth.

"Are you ready?" Static hissed and crackled at the other end sending chills up and down his spine. He gulped.

"Yes elder."

"Tomorrow at the bridge. Midnight." The voice rang out against the crackling static on the call before it hung up with a distant dial tone beeping on and off.

The vampires are here.

A New Beginning

- -

A/N: So sorry for the late update but I come back with great news more updates this week. For those of you wondering what happened to "The Island" it's almost out in stores. I finally got a publishing contract and they accepted my manuscript I would appreciate any of your support the links to the book will be out when my assistant tells me they're out for online retail. Thank you for the long wait on this chapter more to come!

I have a secret. You have to promise me you won't tell anyone because if you do, my life could be in mortal danger. My name is Lark.

I'm a teenager. And a human. But that is not entirely my secret, I'm gay and I am currently living with a vampire.

Just a few months ago I was just barely slipping by with trying to pass my classes and figuring out a future for myself. Little did I know, that I already had a future planned out for me. I was internally worried about leaving the werewolf's at home and joining the dark forces of the vampire realm.

I never seen other vampires before and I'm surprised to learn that they all look human. Like werewolves do, only vampires don't even shift. Or do they? The car drives was long and silent filled with bumpy holes in the road as we drove along the track.My hands felt clammy and my throat felt dry as cotton. I wonder if he could hear how fast my heart was beating or how nervous I was?

"Yes, I can." I jumped in the seat.

"What?" I blurted out. Shocked.

"I'm sorry I didn't mention this to you before but we can hear thoughts, feel your emotions more on amplified level. Like the dogs can."

This means I got to be more careful with what I'm thinking then."Yes, you do."

Please do not answer to my thoughts out loud. I fired at him with a glare making him respond with a throaty chuckle.

"I apologize if that shocked you. I should have mentioned it earlier to you when we first meet."

"I know it's hard for you to understand our world Lark." Tanaka hummed softly under his breath.My mouth felt dry like cotton when he did that sound. It sounded threatening and it left a heavy silence in the air.The room around was still nothing could be heard except for the pang of my beating heart and the sweat tickling down the back of my neck. My eyes were glued on the winding road in front of me nothing but the vast trees that hovered over the 2022 Volvo could be seen.

"I'm glad you know this car as well."

Tanaka murmured as he moved his hand to the radio and switched it onto ACDC. I tsked, arched forward and slapped his hand away and changed it to a different station with classical music.

"Interesting. Classical."

I nodded, better than modern rock I noted in my head. Knowing that he can very well hear me. I leaned back in my velvet car seat and felt like a dog leaning out the rolled down window and just felt the breeze flicker against my face."It's summer already." I murmured lowly under my breath, in a way I was glad I was away from the werewolves. My dad and I always fought about all the little things. Being with the Japanese man changed my perspective on things.

I didn't care if he could hear what I was thinking or not this time I kept that bit to myself.

"Lark...there is something you should know about the Waverly clan." I arched a brow and glanced at him from the corner of my eye.

"Each of us are not well liked around the city."

"Why's that?" I asked.

"We are different from the mortals and the wolves each of us have certain abilities that we can create."

"Abilities?"

"We...we can manifest things into our lives the harder we think about a situation and let go of the intention." I felt my face get pale and my mouth get dry at the thought.

"It's called manifestation abilities. Some of us can manifest something to our lives by just thinking about it in our heads what we think we can create. Thought shifter in a way."The sky above me looked like the color of a cat's vomit as the golden sun turned fuller into hues of purple, grey and black.

Pale skin touched against the soft leather fabric of the veichle.

"We are almost there." He mentioned with a grunt. And we were. There behind the tallest hills and behind the highest bushes and bustle of green trees was Waverly Manor.

My eyes widened like sockets as I saw the famous Japanese cherry blossom tree in the corner. That was the same tree that was rumored to strike when lightening crashed against the blue sky covered with a blanket of clouds. The manor was big, with large class windows covered all over the high building. On each end of the front of the palace stood gargoyles guarding the haunting manor.

"There are only three of us living here myself included." He warned as the Volvo screeched to one side as it hit a dent on the road making me wince at the impact.

"We have four wings in the manor. The west, the east, north, and the south wing. We only have one rule for you thought and that is to not go into the west wing."

"What's in the west wing?" I asked carefully.

"I cannot say for your safety."

I licked my suddenly dry lips.

"They've already been feed. So don't worry about it if you think they will feed on you." My breath stopped and got caught in my throat. "W-what?"

"We feed on human donated blood in the hospitals." My widened the wind picked up its speed and the sun glared down on us the closer we got to the manor.

On the inside, however, I secretly felt jealous that Tanaka fed off of someone else's blood that wasn't my own and I don't know why. Was that wrong? I ignored that thought and batted it away as quickly as it entered my head. I felt the car come to smooth stop as we passed through the rocky pavement in front of the freshly polished marble gargoyles.And I instantly felt like a small human in comparison to the grandor of the manor where lights emoted from the large see through windows.

When he parked the car and came to my side to open it, I slowly stepped out on it with one foot after another. I got out and he shut the door behind me with a small bang and pressed the key and let it lock with a beep. As we took our slow steps up the winding stair case the front doors opened instantly with a creak making my breath shudder underneath me. He went ahead as if it was normal and paused when he realized that I wasn't following him. I looked at his leather jacket and smoothed hair with a stunned expression on my face.

"Come on, you will get used to that." He breathed, beckoning me to enter with a nudge of his hand. "It's part of my abilities, I can make the door open like that." I nodded solemnly and walked inside trailing after him. Instantly my jaw dropped at the glandor inside the manor. It felt like I was inside a mall.

Chandeliers hung on the red walls there was black and white checkerboard floor with black winding stair case.

This was...Waverly manor.

"Who is the human you brought?" A voice boomed from the darkness above the stairs making me jump.

"Althazar." Tanaka warned under his breathe.

"I can easily smell him down the living room in a flash a pale woman with long red hair trailing down her back flashed her way forward in front of me making me feel like a fish out of water.

"Enid, don't hover him." Tanaka pressed his fist clenched to a side.

"We'll see what Artemis has to say about this. Is he a snack you brought for us?"

A snack?

"I smell dogs on him." Everyone fell silent around us and I shrieked into his side. My hands turning cold, the room around me turning a degree colder than it was. The window curtains dancing against the chilly wind that sent goosebumps on my pale skin rising.

I can only hope that none of them wanted to drink my blood alive.

www.ingramcontent.com/pod-product-compliance
Lightning Source LLC
Chambersburg PA
CBHW070400200726
48294CB00003B/1012